TankWitch

Second Edition

W.C. HATOUNIAN

Copyright © 2017 W.C. Hatounian.

This is a work of fiction. All of the characters, names, incidents, organizations, and dialogue in this novel are either the products of the author's imagination or are used fictitiously.

ISBN: 978-1-6772-7127-6 (sc)

ISBN: 978-1-6772-7127-6 (e)

Because of the dynamic nature of the Internet, any web addresses or links contained in this book may have changed since publication and may no longer be valid. The views expressed in this work are solely those of the author and do not necessarily reflect the views of the publisher, and the publisher hereby disclaims any responsibility for them.

Any people depicted in stock imagery provided by Thinkstock are models, and such images are being used for illustrative purposes only. Certain stock imagery © Thinkstock.

Rev: 03/07/2024

To my wife Maggie for all her support and love while

I wrote all my books. Her

Inspiration and enthusiasm were

priceless

This Book is her favorite

Contents

´Chapter I

D oug Baker walked out to the faculty parking lot after his last class amid the milling students trying to get to their cars. He thought it reminded him of an army post after a Saturday morning formation. Doug looked up at the sky; *It looked like it would rain.*

That thought triggered another memory he'd preferred to forget but couldn't remove from his mind. The recollection filled his consciousness, and he couldn't stop the vision from swirling into his mind's eye. He remembered the rain falling so hard that the drops hurt his skin and stung his hands and face as if it were yesterday.

The moonless night had brought on an eerie obscurity he had never experienced before. His poncho had retained more water inside it than repelled, soaking his uniform through sweat and rainwater. Doug sat shivering inside his tank, waiting . . and waiting. Then, from out of nowhere, came an unexpected artillery barrage. He felt the earth explode around him like mini volcanic eruptions. It continued to do so relentlessly. He knew that the ears of every person in the vicinity throbbed in pain from concussions. Their heads ached, and their hands trembled, like his were doing now. He knew what came next.

Baker heard the infantry captain's radioman call for flares through his helmet. He listened to the 4.2-inch mortars lob illumination rounds into the black sky in less than a minute. The heavy rain made their luminescence opaque. The radio blared, "Open fire!"

Through his periscope, Doug watched a compound of American soldiers and tanks unleashing their lethal force on the mass of North Vietnamese soldiers attacking them. The dim light of the flares made the enemies' silhouettes look unnatural as they moved toward them.

Their unique pith helmets easily identified them. Reluctantly, Doug accepted that the Americans' ambush had become compromised. Twenty-year-old Doug Baker felt the recoil as he fired the canister round. The loader had slammed into the breach of the main gun, turning the tank into a 90-millimeter shotgun.

Hundreds of pellets burst from the muzzle and spread from point-blank range. The pellets hacked a swath through the enemy formation, ripping the flesh off their bones like a school of piranha.

At that moment, Doug's mind flashed to the time he went dove hunting with his father back home in Colorado Springs . . . but this wasn't remotely like that. Doug heard someone call for artillery at the command post on an alternate radio frequency. From miles away, the fire direction center replied they had a higher priority and couldn't provide fire support at the moment. He knew the captain's fate rested with his single battery of mortars, which did not hold off this massive counterattack by the North Vietnamese Army, known as the NVA.

He could visualize the panicked mortar crews hurriedly lobbing rounds against an enemy of an unknown number. Not since he had seen it in a drive-in movie could Doug remember a downpour of artillery as intense as this. In a war film he once saw, the mass of enemy soldiers had come at him from the screen; now, it was in person. Doug focused on his job and quickly dismissed the memories.

Doug had listened intently to his lieutenant's words earlier when he briefed the platoon on the upcoming mission for this evening. "Battalion HQ received orders this morning from Brigade S3 (operations) to put a plug into the infiltration route the North Vietnamese Army uses to bring in men and supplies from Cambodia.

"The operations officer has planned an ambush with one infantry company and a platoon of tanks and artillery support. We expect to engage small concentrations of enemy infiltrators."

Doug, like everyone else, had expected to engage a much smaller force of infiltrators. He watched his platoon of five tanks continue to unleash canister rounds against a determined enemy. Their sappers moved in and took the tanks out with rocket-propelled grenades, or RPGs, a Russian-built antitank weapon. Doug knew the American soldiers were taking heavy casualties from what was happening around him. The NVA had several advantages. They had artillery, and the Americans didn't. The NVA also seemed to have a numerical advantage over the Americans. The weather prevented any air support from arriving to support the beleaguered unit.

Finally, Doug heard the captain order the company to collect the wounded and withdraw. Doug, nevertheless, continued to fire into the NVA. A sapper got close enough to shoot an RPG into Doug's tank, but his aim was off, and the antitank round struck the engine compartment. Instead of killing the crew, it destroyed the engine and ignited the fuel lines. A fire quickly spread around the tank and lit up everything and everyone around it.

Doug heard his tank commander, a sergeant, order the crew to abandon the tank. The hatches flew open, and Doug climbed out behind his commander. He saw the driver escape through the driver's hatch and get shot down by the quickly advancing enemy. He watched the same fate befall the loader, who left the tank through another turret hatch.

Doug and the other surviving crewmen joined the retreating soldiers. They watched others continue to fall victim to murderous enemy fire. Doug ran through the jungle, trying to follow the GIs, armed only with a .45-caliber pistol. He'd lost sight of his tank commander.

As the NVA overran the American ambush position, Doug looked behind him, and, in the light reflected by the burning tanks, he saw the enemy shooting the American wounded. Fear gripped him by the throat.

He gasped for air, running, falling, crawling through the slippery vegetation, scrambling to get far away from the enraged enemy. It rained harder. The enemy's flares dimly lit the way in front of him.

The noise was so intense that he could hear nothing else. When he came upon a river, he remembered crossing earlier. Doug knew he was heading in the right direction. Doug had run track in the rain once in high school to show off. He'd caught the flu for his troubles. Now, Doug ran for his life. He crossed the river and tried to crawl up the embankment, but he could get no traction with his boots, and he felt himself sliding back down.

The unmistakable sound of AK-47s ripped the surrounding ground. Terrified, he realized people were shooting at him. His head darted left and right, looking for something to grab onto for support. His heart pounded like a jackhammer.

He felt a sting in his left leg and left shoulder. The fear and adrenaline temporarily masked any actual pain. Doug finally got to the top of the embankment and crawled a few yards through the jungle before he felt it was safe enough to stand. He turned right. Doug thought he was heading toward the road his unit had traveled on. He believed the road would take him toward the American firebase if he found it.

Doug felt his way through the darkness. He knew the enemy wanted to find him and was determined to remain free, but they'd traveled faster than him. Doug inadvertently fell in among them as they traveled through the dark, dense jungle, heading in the same direction he was running. When he stumbled over a pith helmet, he put it on his head to blend in with the enemy.

The monsoon rain stopped as quickly as it started, and the sky cleared. Doug slipped through and around the enemy soldiers and eventually found a clearing. A quarter moon and starlight lit the low, grassy area. His common sense and the will to survive dictated that it would be more prudent to go around the clearing than across it if someone was watching.

His fears kept distracting him. He knew he should pay more attention to where he was walking. Then, without warning, he felt a sharp pain instantly spread throughout his skull. He fell from consciousness and never saw the thick, low-hanging tree branch that had knocked him out.

In the blackness of his mind, his past raced back to him. Doug saw his mother making breakfast, preparing his father's lunch pail, and dressing him for school. He saw his sister come along in other sequences, saw his uncles and aunts, and revisited family trips and vacations.

Doug saw the looks on his parents' faces when he enlisted. Memories swam around his dazed mind like a swirling typhoon. Like vegetation rotting in the humid air, the smell of the ground filtered up through his nostrils, and he realized he was awake. He heard birds singing. Slowly opening his eyes, he saw birds as they lazily traipsed from tree branch to tree branch.

He saw the daylight peeking at him through the tropical forest. The sun's warmth felt good against his battered face. Taking stock of his senses, he wiggled his fingers and toes. He cautiously moved his head and looked around. Nothing immediately aroused his suspicions, so he rolled onto his stomach and felt pain in his left arm. Doug crawled away from the clearing and around behind the tree that had felled him the night before.

Slowly and carefully, he got on his knees and immediately felt the pain from a wound in his left leg. He pulled aside the clothing covering his wounds and discovered flesh wounds, but they'd cut deep trenches through his skin. He knew he needed medical attention soon to avoid getting a nasty infection. Doug had walked for nearly an hour when he heard voices in the distance ahead of him.

They weren't speaking English. Immediately, he looked for a place to hide, but he didn't see one. The voices grew nearer. Panic set in. He crawled into the low bushes, trying to conceal himself. The trees were thin and sparse, the ground flat. He drew his weapon.

Four NVA soldiers walking abreast passed by him. The nearest to him spotted him, but Doug shot him in the head with his .45 before he could alert the others. Then he shot the next man in line. Doug crawled on his belly, grabbed the dead soldier's AK-47, and took the two grenades from his belt. The dead man's eyes stared at him.

The other two soldiers dropped to the ground, expecting an ambush of Americans rushing toward them. None came, and they didn't return fire. Doug slowly crawled over to the other two men's left side. As he neared them, he heard them whispering and saw them. He ensured the AK-47 was off safety, aimed into the taller grass, and opened fire with two short bursts of automatic fire.

The remaining two NVA soldiers died instantly. Doug stripped the dead soldiers of as much ammunition as he could carry and drank the water from their canteens.

Then he continued toward where he believed the American firebase to be. For the next three days, Doug traveled without food and water. He used his escape and evasion training, carefully avoiding NVA patrols and local villages that might be sympathetic to the soldiers. Once Doug felt clear, he looked for any landmark he could identify. Eventually, he saw one. It was a cemetery; he remembered it was on a path near his base camp.

He hurried toward it. Doug walked quickly and with some difficulty because of his leg wound. The road went through the small village and across the road outside his base camp. Excited at finally arriving at his company area, Doug went immediately to his operations shack and reported to the first sergeant. He shared in the excitement and joy of his comrades when they saw him walk through the door alive.

The first sergeant took him to the medics so they could tend his wounds. Later, Doug gave the intelligence officers a complete account of what he'd seen and what had happened. Lying in his bunk, Doug stared at the ceiling and dreaded every day of the remaining three months of his tour.

His experience caused him long, sleepless nights. He dreamed of getting caught and tortured and awoke a few times in a sweat. Even though the dreams subsided, Doug could still feel the fear, anguish, and now all of life's uncertainties around him. At other times, he had feelings of helplessness he couldn't shake.

As the days passed, he kept the scars bottled up inside. He knew he'd never talk of them to anyone, even after he got home and felt safe. But they would never leave the inside of his soul. All he thought of was home. Doug knew his short-timer's irritability clouded his senses and judgment. When he shaved in the mornings, he saw the lost innocence in his craggy face as he looked at himself in the mirror.

The growth and maturity put him way ahead of his biological age, bringing out the sadness in his eyes. He felt nothing for humanity. His emotions were numb from the intoxicating liquors of war and death.

He dreaded his return home. A blaring car horn forced Doug back into reality, his life today, and the need to move on. He glanced around to get his bearings and drove toward his home.

′Chapter II

Vinnie slumbered within his typically sordid bedroom on the second floor of the modest, middle-class home that belonged to his parents, Paul and Mary Bolla.

The windup, black alarm clock on the nightstand ticked, ticked, ticked closer to the obnoxious moment when the subconscious creeps into its dawning awareness of the early part of a new day. Then, at the right moment and with the audacious power of a blaring naval Klaxon in his ear, the recipient is immediately and rudely brought to full, conscious reckoning.

Hovering over his head, the little Irish gremlin named Murphy looked down at poor Mr. Lawrence Vincent Bolla. He was called "Vinnie" most of his life by his family and friends, but he had now grown into a twenty-four-year-old man. Vinnie, the youngest of three siblings, slept in a swirling confluence of alcohol endorphins within a black mind space. Murphy fondly recalled that during Vinnie's young, dawdling years. He had often played an animated stand-in for standard, realistic plastic or rag dolls while his two older sisters . . . now married and with families of their own . . . engaged in the age-old game of playing "house."

Most of these dolls rested in an oak hope chest in their bedrooms. They were all sizes, shapes, and colors, enough to satisfy any growing female's pretentious fantasies. From their perspective, Vinnie appeared similar in size to the toy dolls . . . so the girls figured, why not use the real thing?

Vinnie was too young to realize that flowing within every little girl lives the perpetual dream of the future life; she will live in a Camelot world with all the young knights. She imagines that prince charming will swoop in and take her hand in marriage, and she would take him in bondage . . . a fate yet unknown to the lucky suitor.

The reason is that all little girls are, by far, much more advanced in the arts and techniques of the homemaker. They adopt the marriage-mate mentality when they have their first menstrual cycle. Their unsuspecting male counterpart has spent all his prepubescent time engaging in the testosterone-activated bustle of playing war, baseball, or showing off in front of girls.

Vinnie was far from surrendering his oat-sowing sprees for the bonds of commitment in any form, thanks to the lessons he'd learned by watching his sisters in rehearsal. During their dating years, Vinnie had received regular lectures from his mother, who preached, "This is what you can expect someday when you start dating girls."

Inside Vinnie's mind, the words "No, thanks" rang like the bells of Notre Dame swung back and forth by the hands of Quasimodo.

Like most prepubescent boys, Vinnie had yet to be attracted to girls until one day when a neighbor girl invited him to play "doctor." They entertained each other inside her treehouse. Vinnie soon realized that not all things about girls were bad.

Little did Vinnie know that, at that moment, he'd ventured upon the one anatomical part of the female body that's caused so much devastation to fame, fortunes, careers, and civilizations throughout history, a truth he'd learn soon enough.

Vinnie spent Friday night with his on-again-off-again girlfriend, Angela Moretti, or "Gela," to her family and close friends. She was twenty-one years old, tall, and slender with jet black, naturally curly hair that hung to her shoulders.

Her large, dark brown eyes pierced and probed a man with very determined intent when she considered getting married to him a possibility. Gela, an Italian-American, displayed the typical Italian-American princess traits Vinnie had seen and fallen victim to at his sister's and mother's hands.

Mothers had maternally built insecurity into young daughters. They believed something was wrong with you if you didn't get married and bring forth a son-in-law for the family to feed upon by a certain age. He called it the "you-need-children-for-fulfillment" syndrome.

His mother and aunts had repeatedly hammered at Vinnie, wailing, "If you're not married by twenty-one, a mark will be upon you." His sisters had experienced the same diatribe. But the moment the pronouncement of the vows had left their mouths, and as they raced off into marital bliss, all thought of marks and deadlines mysteriously evaporated. Vinnie knew his family loved Gela.

At least, the women folk felt Vinnie needed Gela to motivate him to do upgraded things, such as improving his life. This natural expectation emanated from Vinnie's parents. Both Vinnie's father and Gela's father, Tony, understood and sympathized with Vinnie's plight and resistance to making commitments.

Like genuine Italian males, the three silently expressed an understanding of the ways of the women. Gela, however, did not understand Vinnie. They had dated intermittently for two years, depending on Gela's monthly mood swings, which seemed unnaturally induced. It continued with her mother's subtle lectures on the finer points of marriage, having children, etc.

Vinnie maintained a resistant attitude toward the relationship. Gela continued to hold faith in it. Over those two years, she and Vinnie shared important holidays, special events, and family get-togethers. Then they'd break up again after things went smoothly for a while.

In Vinnie's mind, this fantasy resulted from Gela's images of shooting stars and the butterflies beaming from her eyes, supported by maternal prodding. Vinnie visualized vampires and Valkyries. Vinnie and Gela always seemed to reconcile when their hormonal levels overrode their better judgments, usually initiated by Vinnie's behavior. It was a classic love-hate relationship.

While Vinnie was growing up, certain people affected the young boy's life. His uncle Andy, for one, developed into a hero figure for Vinnie. Andrew Marco, Vinnie's mother's youngest brother, had distinguished himself during the Vietnam War. Vinnie recalled uncle Andy's influence throughout his emergent years.

Andy acted like a big brother to him, saving Vinnie many times from his broom-riding, banshee-breathed sisters' attempts to eviscerate Vinnie's manhood. Sometimes, as Vinnie listened intently to some of Andy's wartime exploits during his Vietnam tour, he slowly toyed with serving his country in combat.

So, when he came of age, Vinnie felt he should present himself for the common good . . . to protect the Constitution and the Bill of Rights, where all men are created equal, except in the eyes of women, who usually have a terrible habit of separating the men from the boys and of making life generally unequal.

Vinnie joined the Colorado Army National Guard and got assigned to "C" Company, 1st Battalion, 143rd Armor . . . a tank unit . . . out of respect for, and much to the chagrin of, uncle Andy. Vinnie went to Fort Knox for training like uncle Andy had before him.

Once he became a schooled and trained tanker, Vinnie qualified to drive, load, and fire the main gun of an M60A3 main battle tank. He even hit a target with the first round on rare occasions.

Uncle Andy was proud of Vinnie's accomplishments and dedication to his principles. Andy couldn't fault his nephew for doing the same thing he'd done at a time that now felt like a generation ago.

When the Persian Gulf War came, Vinnie got very excited and prayed that his unit would get sent overseas along with their parent regular army unit. They had received their alert order for deployment. Gela's attempts to get Vinnie to marry her increased significantly, fueled by her mother's wailing chorus of "the shadows of spinsterhood." It wasn't any less intense on Vinnie's end. He needed a war to escape these demands of self-imprisonment at home.

Alas, the unit didn't get called, and everything returned to normal, except Vinnie's disappointment in not becoming an actual warrior, which he would never overcome. So, Vinnie turned his energies to his college work and concentrated on finishing his bachelor's degree in boredom.

Reality slowly ticked itself into consciousness on a Saturday morning in October 1991. National Guard drill day (a term used to describe the weekend warriors' activities when they assemble to train) awaited him. On this fine, sunny morning, Specialist Fourth Class Bolla and his crewmembers were taking their M60A3 main battle tank, christened "Victoria Regina," into simulated battle on the live-fire tank gunnery range.

On this day of all weekend drills, the annual qualification of the tank and crew arrived. It arrived every year, a requirement set to test the readiness and mettle of everyone and everything. This mission meant spending the weekend bivouacked in the field, the army's idea of camping, at Fort Carson.

As he awoke, Vinnie's mind edged foggily toward semi-consciousness. His brain slowly embarked on painfully recalling Friday night's adventure with Angela. Every date with Angela was an adventure because you never knew what device she'd used to set a commitment ambush. However, the previous night, Angela had been civil. She hadn't pulled one trick from her black bag. She and Vinnie had a great time at a party at Gela's girlfriend, Sharon's, apartment.

Vinnie had imbibed too much, and Gela took his car keys away and drove him home. She had then walked the short three blocks to her home.

Vinnie's parents, already asleep for hours, would never know how their son's girlfriend had carefully deposited him on their doorstep in those wee hours.

Nor would they know of the whisper Gela had blown into Vinnie's inert left ear, vowing someday to use this incident of humanitarian doorstep-pouring to her advantage. This Saturday, a day ordained and filled with events destined to go wrong . . . especially for those few who needed or expected everything to go off correctly . . . disaster befell Vinnie's alarm clock.

On his way to demolish the finer workings of daily life for people worldwide, Murphy occupied Vinnie's alarm clock. The National Guard expected Vinnie to be at the armory, standing tall in the morning formation by 0730 hours. He didn't know that fate had intervened against him today. Typically, he took thirty minutes to get out of bed, complete the three S's, and then get on the road. Then it takes another twenty minutes to drive to the Penrose armory from his Cañon City home.

The clock had just hit 6:37 a.m. when Vinnie's mother happened by his room, observed the door halfway open, and looked in on Vinnie. To her dismay, she found Vinnie sprawled, half-clothed, over his still-made bed. Mary knew this Saturday constituted one of Vinnie's drill weekends . . . a daily reminder symbolized by the large red circle around the date on the family calendar posted on the refrigerator door. Dismissing any logical reason for Vinnie's current sleeping attire, Mary leaned over and shook his right shoulder. His head flip-flops like a mop to the left and right.

"Vinnie, get up. You're late for your drill . . . c'mon, wake up. It's twenty-to-seven. Don't you have to be there by seven-thirty?"

His mother's warning about the time slowly seeped through his semi-consciousness. Vinnie cocked his right eye and spied the clock Murphy had crapped on. Unable to focus on the time as his brain sloshed back and forth inside his skull because of dear ol' mom's motion on his shoulder, Vinnie rolled over, rubbing his eyes.

"Okay, Mom . . . okay, I'm up," Vinnie whimpered. Mary retracted her hand slightly, suspecting one of Vinnie's old "I'm up" ploys. But this time, when he focused on the clock, Vinnie felt the realization of the lateness of the hour slam into his brain circuits . . . which were devoid of electrolytes, diminished by the alcohol from the night before.

Another part of his brain had triggered, shooting a message to his adrenal gland, which pumped blood and life into Vinnie's hungover body. This realization put a small but significant fire under his droopy ass. At 7:11 a.m., Vinnie peeled out of the driveway after only completing two of the three S's and dressed in his BDUs. *It's a darn good thing I packed my car with my field gear last night before taking Angela out.* He thought.

'Chapter III

ouglas Baker anxiously looked at his watch again. The time now read 07:37 hours, and Vinnie, his platoon's best driver, still hadn't shown up. *Where the hell is Vinnie? He always arrives on time for drills, sometimes five to ten minutes early.*

Baker, the platoon sergeant, and tank commander, had taken a chance and covered for Vinnie, not announcing Vinnie's absence to the lieutenant in the morning formation. This act did not go unnoticed by Specialist Fourth Class Bailey Gunn and Jefferson Boswell (Boz) Wakefield, the other two crewmembers.

Shortly after Doug returned to the United States and officially discharged from the army, he joined the Colorado Army National Guard to earn extra money while attending college. After graduating, he worked as a Cañon City High School history teacher. Doug knew he needed to reinforce his teaching credentials to advance with the school board. He immersed himself in a night school program for the next few years. Doug earned a master's degree in education and a Ph.D. in ancient history.

He paced apprehensively back and forth on the armory floor, mulling over his thoughts. *I'm getting too old for this. I'll be eligible soon for my twenty-year letter. Get promoted to master sergeant, do a year more, and retire.*

I'm looking forward to trying for that school district administration position within the school board, which I expect to open. With my credentials, I foresee little competition. My superiors assure me I have an excellent shot at it and a handsome raise.

Watching where the officers assembled, Doug remembered that the order of the day required the company to leave the armory at 0800. The armory was at the far north end of Penrose. Their equipment sat sixteen miles away on the Fort Carson military reservation. Doug knew he had to ensure his platoon had loaded on the bus on time and get to where the unit parked the tanks.

The movement order called for driving the tanks to the range. The soldiers loaded the tanks the night before with their basic ammunition load. The civil service people who worked there full time refueled the tanks earlier that morning. By following the dirt road, the company would arrive at the entrance gate of the battlefield maneuver and gunnery range. . . a long, bumpy, twenty-five-mile trip. At 0800 hours, Doug's company commander ordered the officers and enlisted personnel to board the buses. Captain Jacob Dillon, a Fort Knox Officer Candidate Program or OCS graduate, was not a veteran of any armed conflict. Doug often wondered how Dillon, who lived and dressed like the consummate, competitive, ego-driven "yuppie" and worked for an engineering firm, made it into the army.

Doug had heard through the grapevine that Dillon had sent his five-ton ammunition trucks on the pretext that the company had arrived and bivouacked on the range to draw the ammunition from Fort Carson's Ammo bunkers the day before the drill weekend.

When the first sergeant heard the rumor, he reminded Captain Dillon it was strictly against regulations to pre-arm combat fighting vehicles. They had to be on the gunnery range inside the Fort Carson military reservation after conducting all safety inspections beforehand.

As Doug recalled, the captain told the first sergeant he planned to hit the range "locked and loaded" and be in position before the Bravo, or B, Company this time. He intended to show that smug, rodent-looking ROTC company commander what a real tank company could do.

The first sergeant, not wanting to impede "Jake the Snake." . . who seemed bent on self-destruction . . . merely shrugged and walked away, mumbling under his breath, "I warned you." Doug understood that Captain Dillon wanted severely to impress the battalion commander. The rodent-faced commanding officer of Bravo Company had embarrassed him the previous month by letting it slip to the colonel that Dillon's recruiting and retention program had not been "up to snuff" this year.

Looking with dismay toward his two juvenile captains and their attempts to outdo one another with very unimpressive behavior, Colonel Oscar Byers, who had served in Vietnam, had become disappointed. The sergeant major, aided by the company's first sergeants, had not tried to stop this nonsense. Amusingly, Doug knew the sergeant major was fond of Lieutenant Colonel Byers. He kept a tight leash on the senior NCO's attempts to find humor in the similarity between the colonel's name and a commercially known and popular brand of hotdogs. The sergeant major once told Doug these two twerp captains did not feel predestined to make the National Guard a home for themselves. Their pettiness eventually caused the Colonel to cut their gonads off when he'd had enough of them.

Now, besides himself, because Vinnie had missed the bus, Doug hoped Vinnie had enough brains to drive to the compound. Bailey's call to Vinnie's home assured Doug that Vinnie had left his house and was en route to the armory and not AWOL.

By 0815 hours, Doug's bus pulled into the compound. A heavily secured enclosure with a double-depth, chain-link fence perimeter surrounded forty acres with barbed wire. Inside stood a maintenance facility supply shed, a headquarters building, and the tank park. It also housed a private security detail to keep trespassers away. The crew dismounted the bus and casually walked to their respective tanks with their gear.

Doug's tank had C31 marked on it, which stood for C Company, Third Platoon, first tank, designating the platoon sergeant's tank. Doug had named the tank Victoria Regina, or "Vicky," because she looked old but regal in her forest camouflage paint.

Doug checked the logbook to ensure that his tank was operationally ready. The logbook outlined Vicky's history from the day she first rolled off the assembly line at the Chrysler tank factory at the intersection of Van Dyke and Twelve-Mile Road in Detroit in 1968 as an M60A1. She had received an upgrade to the A3 version in 1980.

Depending on government funding, the unit did not expect to see the new M1 Abrams Main Battle Tank until the late 1990s or early 2000s. When they initially conceived the tank's name, all four crewmen agreed on it. With unrecognized talent as an artist, Boz received permission from Doug to paint a picture along the side of the main 105-millimeter gun tube.

It depicted a young, pretty woman dressed somewhat like Snow White, wearing a jewel-encrusted crown and flying at a forty-five-degree angle. She held a magic wand in front of her, discharging a thunderbolt. The picture ran the length of the gun barrel. As preparations neared completion for departure, Doug's anxiety increased even further. He walked behind the tank where the two other crewmen stood and said, "Bailey, take over for me. I will see if I can delay our departure until Vinnie shows up. While you're at it, draw our CAR-15s and personal sidearms, and don't forget the ammunition."

"Okay, sarge, we'll get the weapons and let you know when Vinnie gets here if you're not back."

Boz climbed inside the tank and retrieved the weapon's cards, DA Form 3749. Knowing this was a qualifications weekend, the crew had hidden their weapons cards in an envelope under the radio since the last drill. There had never been a time when they'd taken the tank without drawing their small arms.

Boz and Bailey walked over to the small arms armory, drew their four CAR-15s and four Beretta 9-millimeter model 92F semiautomatic pistols, and placed them in their tanker holsters and belts. The crew never used the Berettas unless they qualified. Doug insisted everyone carry their own Colt model 1911 .45 semiautomatic pistol. He and the crew had smuggled them in every drill when they went into the field.

Doug was fond of his crew. To him, they were like the sons he'd always wished he had. Doug knew all about them and their families. Jefferson Wakefield was the same age as Bailey and Vinnie. Boz came from the same middle-class upbringing and suffered from the same non-directional afflictions as they did . . . but he had very interesting talents.

Boz loved mathematics. His hobby entailed figuring out equations from basic algebra to Euclidean geometry. He had completed his degree in mathematics even though he felt it held no future. He knew computers could do anything you needed and faster in math.

Doug remembered when Vinnie, Bailey, and Boz were in his high school history class. They knew each other back then and had graduated during the same year. The boys joined the Army National Guard within weeks for their reasons, without telling each other or their other friends.

Eventually, they all ended up in the same armored unit. It exposed their shyness and sheepish feelings of *"Oh, hi. I guess you're bored and confused, but won't admit it or tell anyone."*

Doug marveled at how Vinnie, Boz, and Bailey carefully maneuvered, getting to be crewmembers on the same tank to maintain their camaraderie. As they grew to know each other better, they discovered a shared brotherhood in bondage by anecdotally tormenting older sisters. After weekend drills, they hoisted many a beer to manhood at their local watering hole, Majorettes, in Cañon City.

Boz, at that point content with college, had worked for the mathematics department on a federal grant and loved being a tanker in the guard. It seemed to put a little purpose in his life. Boz's father, the local bank president and a leader in the black community, naturally approved Boz's decision to join the guard.

During the Vietnam War, his father served in the Navy as a petty officer on a gunboat in the Mekong Delta. He felt the same as Bailey's father: *"The service can do a lot for you if you give it a chance."* Boz and Bailey returned to Vicky across the parking lot loaded with weapons and ammunition.

While they walked, Boz put his arm around Bailey's shoulder and said, "If Vinnie was out with Angela last night, I imagine he's either super beaked or happy."

"Yeah, only if he got laid."

"Hey man, there must be more to Angela than her body." Bailey reached for a smoke in his leg pocket.

"Would you put up with her beaking? I don't think so. You'd tell her the same as I would."

"Yeah, and what's that?"

"Take a hike, missy; that's what."

"Oh man, Bailey, you tell that to every woman."

"She's an albatross, Boz. That's why I refer to irksome wives and girlfriends as 'trosses for short. And what does an albatross have? A beak! What do women love to use on a man . . . their mouths to nag, nag, nag ya . . . ergo, you get the beak. They had developed and programmed from the day they're born to beak ya. Little girls have given 'TITs' a new meaning: 'Trosses-In-Training.'"

They laughed and climbed aboard the tank, securing their equipment and weapons. Doug convinced the platoon leader, Lieutenant Moore, that his tank had a minor problem with the diesel engine's fuel injection system that would pose no long-term delay.

He said they'd catch up to him when his crew repaired it. The lieutenant planned to wait and go as an entire platoon, but Doug assured him he'd meet them before the company finished filing through the gate at the range.

Moore bought the story and left for his tank. Doug walked back to Vicky, lost in his thoughts of whether Vinnie had run afoul or something else had prevented him from making it to drill. Bailey and Boz eyed each other and then looked over at Doug.

"I think he's upset 'bout Vinnie," Boz surmised.

"Yeah, so am I. Most of the company has already left, and Vinnie should have been here by now."

"I hope he has a damn good reason, for Vinnie's sake."

"Maybe he had car trouble."

"Maybe he could have called," Doug mumbled as he returned to the tank.

It was 0830 hours, and the last vehicle had left the gate ten minutes before. Doug opened his mouth, ready to tell Bailey to take the driver's seat and crank Vicky over, when Vinnie's blue '68 Chevrolet Malibu slid sideways through the open gate.

He quickly found a place to park, grabbed his gear out of the trunk, and ran toward Vicky before the dust had cleared enough for the three crewmen to see it was Vinnie running toward them, duffel bag in hand. Doug's face contorted.

"Where the hell have you been, Vinnie? Bailey called your house over an hour ago. It doesn't take that long to drive here," he roared.

"I'm sorry, sarge. I...I ran out of gas on the way over." Without success, Vinnie puffed, out of breath, trying to climb aboard Vicky. Boz reached out, grabbed Vinnie's hand, and pulled him onto the fender skirt while Bailey grabbed Vinnie's duffel bag and secured it on the turret bustle with the rest of their bags.

Doug leaned his six-foot, two-inch, 220-pound muscular body over Vinnie's pale, thin, dehydrated face and boomed, "Don't bullshit me, Vinnie . . . that's the oldest excuse in the book."

"Honest, sarge, I did," Vinnie said as he crawled toward the loader's hatch between Doug's legs.

"I gotta hear this," Bailey whispered to Boz.

Vinnie finally got into the driver's seat, strapped himself in, and plugged his helmet in. He turned the battery switch on the driver's master control panel on his right. Bailey and Boz donned their helmets and plugged them into the tank's intercom system. Doug secured himself in the track commander's or TC's seat under the cupola.

Boz took the gunner's position today. He sat inside the tank and in front of Doug while Bailey enjoyed the seat across from Doug, called the loader's hatch. Vinnie kept his driver's hatch open for air. After ensuring the parking brake got set to the ON position, he went through the starting procedure.

He checked and closed the compartment drain valves. Then, set all electrical switches to OFF except for the fuel pumps and heater master; purged the air from the fuel lines by pumping the purge pump handle, pressed the accelerator pedal, and hit the starter button just above the battery switch. The engine came to life.

After waiting a few minutes for the engine to warm up, Vinnie slowly drove Vicky out of her parking space and headed toward the gate. Without warning, Vicky coughed and rumbled to a stop. Vinnie had a hard time keeping her running.

"Now what?" Boz blared.

"Vinnie, what the hell are you doing? You're going to flood her," Doug yelled over the intercom, causing everyone to wince from the sharp pain piercing their eardrums.

"No, I'm not," Vinnie peeped.

"Shut her down and let me look at her," Bailey grumbled.

Doug was grateful to have Bailey there. Because of his knowledge of power plants, he'd pulled their fat out of the fire during field exercises a few times. Bailey fixed Vicky's engine problems himself. He made possible many of the Third Platoon's honors in combat readiness. . . instead of sending the tank to the battalion maintenance REMFs.

REMF is an acronym for full-time government employees who drank coffee off Vicky's engine deck door and then wrote, "Can't duplicate the problem" in her logbook before sending her back. That was a common technique used by the lazy. Then, they'd return to work on their personal projects rather than doing the job they were getting paid by the taxpayers.

Bailey Gunn came from Eurasian extraction. His mother had an English-Spanish background, and his father was of Indo-Chinese and European lineage. Bailey's ancestry gave him a natural, light tan and a hint of almond in the shape of his eyes.

His build mirrored that of a short, thin Asian. Like Vinnie, he had two sisters: one was eighteen going on thirty, and the other was a twenty-six-year-old with a more normal character. The younger sister had caught the eye of many of Bailey's friends, including Vinnie.

But Vinnie could not, with a clear conscience, date this tall, slender, dark-eyed beauty. He knew her reputation for being the commanding, bossy type. Vinnie knew he wouldn't have the stomach to look Bailey in the face if a passionate incident occurred between him and his buddy's sister.

Bailey had the expertise of a mechanical miracle worker. He had worked for his father in the family business.

"The army made a man out of me," the old man had always told Bailey. "Maybe what you need, son, is some leather boot direction."

Doug ordered the crew to open and secure the engine cover door by electrically swinging the turret after moving the main gun out of its travel lock. They undid the screws holding the rear exhaust grate doors in place. Bailey grabbed his personal tool kit, which he'd put together for situations like this, and climbed into the engine compartment.

There sat Vicky's 750-horsepower, 12-cylinder Continental AVDS-1790-2C Engine. Bailey looked at Vinnie and said, "Vinnie, get into your hole and plug in. When I tell you to, crank her over." Vinnie complied, and after an intercom check, he waited for Bailey's command to start Vicky. Bailey checked all the wiring and fuel lines to the injectors.

"Okay, Vinnie, turn her over."

Vinnie turned the master power switch on and hit the Start button. Vicky coughed, sputtered, and came alive again . . . weakly. Bailey checked each line and injector and then the fuel pump.

"We got a broken fuel line," Bailey said finally.

Boz and Doug said in unison, "Great!"

"Vinnie, didn't you do an engine run-up check?"

"Uh . . . no, sarge, I forgot."

Doug looked over at Bailey. "How long?"

"Depends. Thirty minutes, maybe. If it's something worse, it won't matter."

"Boz . . ."

"I know; go check if maintenance has a spare part. I was on my way before you thought it."

"Thanks, Boz."

"Don't mention it," Boz yelled as he trotted toward the double set of garages used for tracked vehicle maintenance while in the field. Sergeant Fred "Filmy Milker" Milkie, who also carried the parts supply sergeant's title, was a mild-mannered, dumpy-looking . . . never-married . . . man in his fifties.

Like many full-time reservists, he waited for when he could draw his civil service pension, milking the system through empire building. Many years earlier, at his first supply post job, Fred had quickly earned the moniker "Filmy Milker" from some Specialist Fourth Class or Spec-4. It was because of his usual lack of basic hygiene, frumpy appearance, and the inability of the Spec-4 to stand in the presence of Fred without a gas mask . . . for which only Fred had the keys.

Not only did the Spec-4 have trouble getting near Fred, but when doing so, the mere sight of Fred reminded him of a caricature of the Sad Sack comic strip. Fred had obtained a civil service job in his supply specialty.

They had transferred him from state to state until someone found him a job at Fort Carson. He was to mind the parts supply store of the 143rd Armor in nowhere land and offended no one.

Boz walked to the parts counter and tried not to gag. Filmy sat behind it, consumed with his favorite magazine, Field and Stream. He'd propped his feet up on his desk for comfort, in the manner befitting a man of his stature.

"Sergeant Milkie, I need a fuel line for our tank; I'll direct exchange (DX) it with you as soon as we get the old one out."

"Where's your paperwork?" Filmy said in a low, soft tone, peering over his bifocals.

"Sergeant Milkie, I don't have any paperwork. The company has already pulled out. We're late, and we need to get outta here."

"Sorry, son, no paperwork, no parts."

"Do you even have the parts?" Boz asked.

"Dunno … can't check until I have a requisition."

"Do you mean to tell me you won't even get up and check until I fill out a form?"

"That's right, son."

"Well, how about if I check for you?" Boz offered.

"Oh, I can't let you do that. That's unauthorized."

"Sergeant Milkie, you do not need paper to DX, an item."

"Don't tell me 'bout the regs. I need the request, and then I'll get you the part."

"But we need the piece now, not a week, a month, or a year from here if you order it."

"Well, I'm sorry, Son. I can't he'p ya."

The crash of the corrugated steel door slamming open caused Boz's knees to buckle and his body to quiver like he was having the scare of his life. He watched Filmy receive the fright of his life as his chair fell from under him. He fell backward, magazine in hand, doing a double roll into the parts bin.

Doug jumped over the counter, picked Filmy off the floor with one hand, and held him about three feet off the ground. Then he slammed him into the screen cage to the right of the parts bin.

Filmy's bifocals slid down the bridge of his nose and hung on by one ear. Doug saw that his eyes, barely visible through his moppy brown and gray hair, shone wide like big silver dollars with no color.

Filmy hung there like a loose sack of straw. He stared in terror into Doug's rabid, snarling red face, a face that looked as if it'd frighten Frankenstein. Doug's eyes seemed ablaze with fire and madness.

"Filmy, I will ask you one question and one question only. Where are the fuel lines kept?"

Filmy, never prone to violence, limply lifted his right hand and weakly pointed his bony index finger to a metal closet against the wall behind Doug. Boz didn't need a cue to jump over the counter. He raced to the cabinet, opened the doors, searched the shelves, and grabbed the appropriate fuel line.

"I got it, sarge," Boz yelled as he bolted through the opening where there had once been a door, now reduced to a twisted mess, like Filmy's insides.

Doug let go of Filmy, who dropped in a disheveled pile to the floor.

Doug walked from the supply room back toward the tank. Bailey and Vinnie had removed the bad fuel line when Boz ran up with the good one.

"Here ya go, Bailey," Boz said as he tossed Bailey the new line.

"Jesus Christ, Boz, this thing is heavy; ya trying to break my fingers?"

When Doug returned to the tank, Vinnie chuckled and was about to chime in with some sarcastic quip.

"Vinnie, get down here; I'm not finished with you," he growled.

Vinnie jumped off Vicky and stood in front of Doug. Boz got in the engine compartment to give Bailey a hand and kept in earshot of the momentous explanation they figured they would get.

"Well, I want to hear this 'out of gas' excuse you have."

"Well, sarge, I got a late start, and while I was on my way along Highway 50, I ran out of gas. I walked back to Florence, and about a mile later, a county Mountie picked me up and drove me to the nearest gas station. I got a five-gallon can and started back. Then a trucker picked me up about . . .oh, I don't know, a few miles up the road . . . and drove me to my car. I filled up the gas tank, and here I am."

Doug's eyes bored into Vinnie's eyes, and he saw the truth in that innocent face. Vinnie had never lied to him, and he had no reason not to believe him now. Doug had a lot of experience observing his students lying to him. Vinnie displayed no deceitful traits.

"I'm going to the latrine," Doug said as he turned to walk off.

Now nearly finished installing the new fuel line, Bailey and Boz peeked out at Vinnie. Vinnie joined Boz and Bailey in the engine compartment.

"Hey, Bailey, isn't that the engine governor's linkage?" Vinnie said, pointing.

The governor was a device intended to limit the tank's speed to thirty-five miles per hour to prevent burning out the drive system. However, many a crew knew how to disconnect it in times of need.

"Since when did you become a mechanic, Vinnie?" Bailey asked.

"Hey, Bailey, I'm not as dumb as I look. I've studied the M60 engine too, ya know."

"Okay, Vinnie, I'm sorry. I was just surprised. I never figured you as mechanically minded."

"I may not know as much as you, but I know a few things. Now, is that the linkage to the governor or not?"

"Yes, it is. What of it?"

"Disconnect it."

"What? Are you crazy? You wanna blow up this tank engine or what?"

"No, dipstick; I only want a few more miles per hour so we can catch up."

"Vinnie, what's in that obtuse mind of yours?" Boz asked.

"I know a shortcut out to the main gate, but I need all the speed I can get. Now, Bailey, you know engines. If it sounds like I'm straining anything, kick me, and I'll slow down. Doug will never know. You can reattach the linkage when we join the company," Vinnie said.

"Oh? You think Doug hasn't disconnected a governor a time or two? You think he won't catch this? I don't know, Vinnie. It's not a good idea. Besides, these engines are mighty funny, and Doug'll kick your ass even if I don't warn you in time," Bailey added.

"If you won't do it, get out of the way, and I will." Bailey saw the determination in Vinnie's eyes.

"Look, guys, it's my fault we're late, and I feel responsible, so I want to make up the lost time and keep Doug's ass out of trouble. He covered for me, and I feel I owe him something."

Bailey couldn't argue with that. He saw the approval on Boz's face.

"Okay, Vinnie, you got it . . . but how will you convince Doug to take the shortcut?"

"You leave that to me."

When Bailey finished installing the new fuel line, he disconnected the governor, turned to Vinnie, and said,

"You know, Vinnie, we could all get into a lot of trouble for doing this."

"Trust me," Vinnie said, hoping to come across convincingly.

Chapter IV

The old hag sat uncomfortably on a three-legged, hand-carved wooden stool in front of the fire pit in her gloomy but roomy damp cave, studying her crystals and reflectors of various sizes and shapes. She studied her face in her pocket mirror. Upon seeing the toll premature aging had taken, she realized her time was nearing.

As she stared into the fire, memories of the many years she exuded great beauty flooded back. She'd been tall and lithe, with long, black hair that flowed and fell to the small of her back. She had delicate features, high cheekbones, almond-shaped catlike green eyes, and a long, slender, regal-looking nose. Her eyes, which once shone at night like an owl, were now dim and hollow with age.

Today, when she looked in the mirror, she saw a cursed woman with a fat and puffy face. She scratched the wart growing on her nose. Her gnarled hands lessened her ability to grip or hold anything. She looked at her blackened teeth in the reflection and saw most nearly gone.

Plumpness shrouded her short body, accented by thinning, frizzy, mousey gray hair. She'd worn long, elegant silk robes in her heyday, overflowing with many colors. She couldn't remember her last birthday, but she knew the village girls came from the hamlets in the valley below each spring and brought her baskets of flowers, dried sweetmeats, fruits, and nuts. They knew and loved her.

Before them, their mothers and grandmothers maintained a grave secret they had passed on to their daughters. If these girls ever needed to hide and find protection, no one could divulge her whereabouts to any man, relative, or friend. If they ever did, they'd cause the death of many, including themselves and the witch.

She remembered when everyone had known her as the sorcerina, Audra. She saw her father, Alberic, the castle sorcerer, and her mother, Mystranna, the sorcerer's wife, as she looked into her crystals. Audra still mourned her mother. Her mother had died when Audra turned fourteen. Mystranna had passed on all her most personal secret spells, curses, and cures to her daughter, even unknown to her husband.

Her father, Alberic, had died when Audra turned twenty. He had also shared his secrets with her, even those his wife wasn't aware of. Audra had dreamed of becoming the realm's queen sorceress until one autumn day when Zenega arrived without invitation or explanation. An older-looking man, he had a balding pate with graying black hair on the sides. He wore a silver-colored scapular.

The pallor of his skin was ashen. Audra felt an evil air radiating from him wherever he went. He'd brought his bodyguard detachment, which he called the Red Guards. Audra always believed that Zenega had cast a spell upon the old king to be named the Kingdom's wizard.

Zenega clarified he intended to have her as his consort, but she'd refused him, and his spells failed to work on her. For a time, they worked separately, and she kept her distance. One day in late October, she noticed a strange thing. During the second fortnight, young girls who had come of age were mysteriously disappearing, one at a time. It continued every year.

Not all the girls disappeared, only a few, enough to frighten everyone in the villages and hamlets. Fate oddly spared girls of means and position who lived inside the castle. Villagers complained to the King about kidnapping their daughters and demanded he do something.

Fearing a revolt, the King called on Zenega and confided in him about his dismay and confusion about dealing with the missing girls. Zenega had no patience with the King's ineptness. To gently persuade the King, Zenega told him of a visit he had received from a "presence" that had made a demand on him.

In his gruff manner, the King refused to be alarmed about demands made on his sorcerer. His only concern was maintaining peace within the realm. Zenega's annoyance with the King triggered a reaction deep within his psyche. He abruptly turned and faced the King, nose to nose. The King felt fear immediately spread throughout his body as he looked at the intensity of Zenega's burning, reddish eyes, contorted face, and snarling mouth.

"During the last fortnight of every October, certain selected young girls are coming of age and must avail themselves as sacrifices. Should anyone attempt to interfere, evil will descend upon the valley. A destroyer will come forth and burn the villages and the crops and kill the cattle," Zenega threatened the King.

The King, horrified and trying not to cringe, warned Zenega that any sacrifice involving children was barbaric, and he forbade it. Therefore, he must thwart this evil presence. Zenega regained his composure and abruptly told the King he had no control over the evil.

Then he walked away. The King headed back to his offices. As he walked, he recalled the castle dwellers mentioning that they had noticed this time of year, a type of madness would come over Zenega. He'd lock himself in his apartment and not come out until his madness passed.

During the third year of Zenega's spells of madness, which Audra was privy to, she stopped the blackmail. She'd found a complex of caves within the hills in the forest, far away from the valley. In July of that year, Audra traveled from village to village. At the grotto near the road at the valley's southern edge, she asked all the girls of age to meet her.

Leading the girls into the hills, she showed them the cave complex, ensuring they knew where to run before the October fortnight. She cautioned them to stay there until the evil time had passed. Audra told the girls to travel in daylight only and never alone.

She warned them to keep this a secret among themselves for their protection. When the October fortnight approached, the girls fled. The evil thing came into the valley, enraged, and took revenge upon the villages. The evil burned huts and crop fields and took cattle. It howled like a dying animal in great pain. It's shrill, causing the people to tremble in their beds and homes. The King and queen and those who dwelt in the castle felt afraid as the immense walls shook and the ground trembled under them.

As hard as Audra tried, some girls disappeared year after year because they left for the hills too late, traveled alone, and got lost. Those few girls never quenched the desires of the evil things. Eventually, Zenega discovered Audra's hand was behind the scheme to save the girls from becoming offerings of sacrifice to the evil.

He went into a fit of rage and swore retribution. He distracted Audra long enough to slip a potion into her wine goblet one day. She saw herself turned into the form that would seize her body and shorten her life. One day, the old king unexpectedly passed on into the afterworld.

After being ceremoniously crowned, the prince immediately married the daughter of a wealthy baron and knight and reigned like an unwitting fool. Zenega convinced the new king that the sorceress Audra bore full responsibility for the rage of the evil during October.

He insisted she pay for her treason and burn at the stake. Upon hearing this, one of the queen's ladies-in-waiting rushed to Audra and warned her. Audra immediately gathered her belongings and fled to the hills to hide when she learned of this abomination and treachery.

Since that day, she had remained in the forest and dedicated her life to caring for the girls every year when they came. Audra knew her only hope rested with someone who would champion her battle against this wrongdoing and stop the sacrifices forever. Perhaps, she thought, if her champion successfully defeated Zenega and his surrogates, it might cause the abnegation of the spell Zenega had unscrupulously cast on her.

Audra sent for many knights, who yearned for a quest by using spells and witchcraft, purposely timing it before October. Audra discovered the evil's location in the Kingdom using her medium through her crystals.

She sent the knights the information with a telepathic signal. The evil bested and devoured the knights. After a time, the new king's guards discovered strange knights roaming the Kingdom and determined their true purpose.

The guards' commanding officer formed a plan to arrest the knights when they entered the valley. Zenega, learning of the strange knights' forays into the realm, warned anyone who attempted to disturb the peace and harmony of the valley, risked causing great peril to the entire kingdom.

Although they were still free, everyone in every village and hamlet felt even more like a captive than before. One day, Audra rested along the brook near her cave and saw a reflection in the water. She leaned over, over-tasking her girth, and reached into the water to pluck out what she would discover to be a strange, spherical object with great difficulty.

She could see through the crystalline object as clearly as through the water it came from . . . but when she shook it, a cloud-like substance formed inside it and would swirl around. When the substance cleared, she saw people in strange places who wore strange clothes and moved around on carts without horses and, sometimes, on objects that flew through the air. She thought that, wherever this place existed, she might find someone to come to her valley, defeat the evil, and save her girls.

On a chilly autumn day, while she sat under an elm tree near her brook gazing at her crystal sphere, she saw four men wearing green clothing that made them look like parts of a tree. They mounted an iron beast with a long snout. Her intuitive instincts told her that the beast she saw was a war weapon. The sphere radiated into her palm, sending her the thought of these men's clothing made up a uniform, since they all wore the same thing.

Overwhelmed by this strange, inexplicable understanding of what she saw, she closed her eyes. In the depths of her mind, she formulated a spell. She focused her thoughts on bringing the men and their iron beast to her. She set about saying the spell aloud, in words her mother taught her for occasions like this. As she rubbed her gnarled hand over the sphere, it slowly turned red and burned, smoking in the palm of her left hand.

Sensing danger, she tossed the sphere into the brook from which it had come before it burned her even more. It exploded into a million tiny pieces when it hit the cold water. Not knowing if her spell had worked, her plan would require her to show patience, optimism, and worry, for the October fortnight was now at hand.

Chapter V

A fter the crew put their coveralls on over their BDUs, got into their positions, put on their helmets, and plugged in, Vinnie cranked Vicky over. She purred like a lion.

While the crew underwent their start-up procedures, Vinnie grabbed the steering T-bar. He put the gearshift lever that extended from his right into drive and stepped on the accelerator, moving the tank from its parking spot to face the main gate.

Boz turned on the turret's power from the gunner's switch box, which sat in front of him to the right, and then he turned on the STAB power switch and checked for an indicator light. Now, the turret had power, along with gun stabilization.

Vinnie backed Vicky toward the headquarters building where Doug had gone earlier. When Doug exited the building, he saw, to his surprise, the tank waiting for him like valet parking delivering your car.

He hadn't expected the crew and Vicky to appear eager to get moving.

Doug climbed aboard Vicky and eased into his seat in the cupola. Vinnie increased the throttle before Doug got his helmet on and drove the tank to the gate, causing Doug to be jerked around in his seat.

"You in a hurry?" Doug barked, strapping his helmet on.

"I'm just trying to move along, sarge," Vinnie replied.

Vinnie made a sharp right turn and settled the tank on the road. He knew the fork was coming along really soon. Vinnie had a reputation among the crew as the embodiment of a smooth talker. He'd proven it with Angela . . . but he knew Doug wasn't Angela.

"Hey, sarge, we're over an hour and a half late; no thanks to me, but I think I can make up the time if you let me take a shortcut."

"What shortcut?" Doug asked with suspicion.

"Well, there's a fork up the road. The right fork goes by the tank trail. The left fork goes to Highway 115. This time of day on a Saturday, no heavy traffic runs on Highway 115, and no one should be on the turnoff to the highway. I can beat Third Platoon to the gate, and we can fall in, and no one will ever know we were missing."

"Vinnie, you know as well as I do we are not authorized to drive this, or any tracked vehicle, on a state highway. We need permission, appropriate support vehicles, and paperwork to go with it."

"I know, sarge, but it's our only chance. Besides, we won't be on the state highway for long, just a few miles, until we make the cutoff back onto the reservation. It's only a few miles. We can be on and off the highway before anyone sees us."

"I don't know, Vinnie; it sounds too risky. What if you get us lost?

Where is this cutoff on Highway 115?"

"It's an old abandoned road about fifteen or twenty miles up the highway that used to go to an amusement park. It closed in the fifties."

"Yeah, I know that road. We used to have dockers out there before the MPs caught us and told the police," Bailey said.

"Isn't there an old rail spur that parallels that road?" Doug asked, still thinking about the consequences of this maneuver.

"That's right. It used to be used by the army for supplies and passenger trains going to the park. The tracks are gone, but the platform and water tower remain." Bailey said.

"We can only get to that road from Highway 115, and it will take us right to the main tank trail, just south of the main fort. There's a gate, and we can get through it without problem 'cause I know the combination."

"Oh, and how, pray tell . . . my fine, influential friend . . . do you know that?" Doug cackled.

"I have a buddy I work with in an MP unit; he told me they never change the combination. I tested it last month when I drove to the PX and needed to get home 'cause I was running late," Vinnie admitted.

"Vinnie, I think that information should be confidential and for military use, not for your personal shortcuts."

"Well, sarge, maybe so, but the point is, it's available, and we need to get ourselves there. Otherwise, we will cause a lot of heartburn when we can't get down range today."

"Yeah, sarge, the lieutenant's depending on you to get Third Platoon a good score, and he will become mighty pissed when he doesn't see your smiling face out there," Boz chimed in to show support for the plan.

"Besides, we're at the fork, sarge," Vinnie stated with finality. Doug took in a deep breath.

True, we are late, maybe even late. I know there is no way we can catch up in time. It's up to me to run the range, according to the lieutenant. The company commander made Moore the range master, meaning I, the noncommissioned officer in charge or NCOIC, needed to make it happen.

The captain had left no doubt and had emphasized his desire to get rounds down range today.

Okay, I know it's risky, but I guess I'll take the chance . . . though it's against my better judgment. Exhaling, Doug said to himself with sardonic amusement.

"Okay, hell, let's go for it! But if we get into a screw-up, it's on our asses because I'm not going down without my best crew."

Doug usually suppressed the hidden, adventurous streak inside him; he hadn't acknowledged it for many years. He painfully recalled that the last time he and a bunch of friends had gotten adventurous, he'd ended up engaged. Shortly after leaving for Vietnam, she'd dumped him for a homeboy. Vinnie hung a left at the fork.

It wasn't a fork but a turn off the main dirt road. Vinnie headed west to the state highway. Ahead, on the roadway, an obstacle reminded him of an adage about what happens when you're in a hurry. A deuce-and-a-half truck, officially known as a "two-and-one-half-ton truck," had run off the same road and got stuck in a ditch filled with mud. Now, half the truck blocked the roadway. The terrain along this stretch ran through hills filled with sycamore trees.

"I thought you said no one would be on this road, Vinnie," Doug said, needling his driver.

With no room to maneuver around the truck, Vinnie stopped the tank. The truck driver and assistant driver did not see the tank approach and became startled when Bailey walked up and asked if they needed any help.

"Yeah, wise guy, ya got a wrecker in yer pocket, Einstein?" Snarled the crusty, old, fatty-assed staff sergeant wearing a newly soiled BDU uniform.

"As a matter of fact, I do, Sergeant; however, I'm not sure if I'll let you use it unless you're polite to me," Bailey beamed.

"Why, you little punk, I'll kick your skinny little ass!" the sergeant growled, coming up off the ground and puffing from the exertion to move his girth from the front of the stuck truck.

When the overweight sergeant approached the truck's rear, he saw fifty-two tons of steel facing him. Three angry men stood on the road looking like they were from a Western movie.

Bailey noted the fat man's look, expressing a classic portrait of disbelief. Vinnie shut off Vicky and dismounted. The other crewmen had overheard the conversation and became equally displeased with the fatty-assed sergeant's response.

Noting that he, an E-6, did not outrank Doug, an E-7, the sergeant immediately changed his caustic tone.

"Ah . . excuse me, men, I'm sorry if I was . . ah . . rude, but we're stuck, and I was . . ah . . .ya know, a bit frustrated. Can ya give us a hand?" He said with a phony smile.

Here's another fine example of real army rear- echelon supply and support personnel. Who's never seen a day of actual combat and gets excited when they're snuck up on? Doug thought.

Doug went to the front of the truck with the fatty-assed sergeant to check out the damage. Vinnie walked to where Boz and Bailey were standing.

"These two mud-wallowers don't seem where they should be," Vinnie observed.

"How ya figure?" Bailey asked.

"As you can read, the markings on this truck indicate an on-post supply unit. So why are these two sneaking around on this old dirt road?" Vinnie questioned.

"Good point," Boz responded.

"Let's snoop," Vinnie suggested.

To his amusement, Vinnie discovered the army truck had no legal dispatch form and no DD Form 1970 in the truck's logbook, which meant it was illegally on the road. The overnight luggage inside the bed showed these two had taken this truck into town without authorization.

They were now trying to sneak it back to the post. While the men hooked the tow cable to the truck, the fatty-assed sergeant attempted to make small talk with Doug until he learned Doug and company belonged to the National Guard. The sergeant's caustic tone returned, and Doug got very annoyed. When Vinnie pulled the truck out of the mud and reattached the tow cable to Vicky, the driver and his partner drove off in the truck without saying thank you. Now, Doug became incensed.

"Vinnie! Crank her over. Everybody mount up, and let's get out of here." Doug said in a strident tone.

All military reservations have on-duty military police patrols that secure the perimeter of the military reservation. Bailey donned his helmet and got on the tank's radio. He set in the FM frequency the MP's use. Bailey called an MP jeep on patrol. He told the military policeman what he had discovered.

He provided the truck's ID number, the road they were on, and their traveling direction, trying to sneak back into the post. After the call, Bailey explained to Doug what they'd found and why he had alerted the MPs.

Doug formed a big grin and yelled at Vinnie, "On, Mc Duff!" Vicky roared to life, and Vinnie poured on the coal.

Since the two goldbrickers had hurried off so quickly, they'd forgotten to secure the gate behind them, and Vinnie drove straight through. Everyone knew they needed to hurry, with only ten miles left to get to the state highway.

Doug absorbed the delightful Colorado autumn of 1991; the trees changing color and the snow accumulating on the distant mountains painted a colorful picture. The crew's weather briefing called for an unusually high-pressure area that would bring some prematurely warm air from the southwest. It would cause the small streams and brooks to fill with runoff water. Ergo, trucks are getting stuck in the mud. It was an enjoyable day to drive with your windows lowered, your convertible top-down, or all your hatches open when riding around in a tank.

Doug took in the fresh air while sitting in his TC's seat and couldn't see inside when Bailey took the bottle of Crown Royal and handed it to Boz, who also sat inside the turret, to hide before Doug saw it.

"Did you take this off the truck?" Boz mouthed.

Bailey nodded. For now, Boz hid the bottle in Bailey's famous first-aid kit until later when he'd get to hide it better.

"Where'd you find it?" He mouthed again.

"In that sergeant's overnight bag; payment for using Vicky," Bailey answered, moving only his lips and pantomiming with his hands. Boz gave Bailey the thumbs-up and went on with his work. Having driven from a lower level, Vinnie reached a higher road elevation.

The distance from the gate to the ridge was now only three miles along an old riverbed. The climb to the plateau took another two miles. Only a straight run remained to the highway, along a wide, flat dirt road surrounded by rolling hills and grasslands. Bailey and Boz sat out on the loader hatch, lost in their thoughts, while Vinnie was determined to catch up no matter what.

Vinnie played Born to Be Wild; he'd jerry-rigged into the tank's communications system and broadcast it into its intercom. He knew everyone liked rock 'n roll music.

Vinnie hoped no one noticed Vicky cruising at forty-five miles per hour and making a high rooster tail of dust. The movement order allowed the tanks to move tactically with their main guns swung around to the front, out of the normal locked-to-the-rear position commonly called the "travel lock."

Doug had allowed the crew to travel tactically before giving the okay to take the shortcut. Therefore, the cupola's hatch cover moved with the turret and opened to the rear. Doug never noticed the heavy dust cloud behind Vicky.

Vinnie saw the embankment coming and slowed down. A cattle guard separated the shoulder of the road and the highway. State Highway 115 was a two-lane, paved road raised off the roadbed a foot or two for water runoff.

Vinnie drove to the edge of the highway, turned right, and positioned the tank parallel to the asphalt road instead of driving on it and then turning it. This procedure prevented the tracks from gouging the asphalt.

Everyone looked around. When Vinnie felt no other traffic was coming behind them, Vinnie drove Vicky onto the road slowly and gradually increased the speed. Now, close to late morning, everyone's anxiety level increased.

Chapter VI

A change in pitch to Vicky's big continental engine brought Doug out of his thoughts. He looked at the highway and noticed they'd gone from open fields and rocky hills to forested countryside. Trees whizzed past him. It didn't feel like they were going thirty-five miles per hour. Doug immediately suspected someone, or a group of someones, had tampered with the engine's governor.

Doug remembered he'd disconnected a governor a time or two himself. He grinned inwardly, but intended not to show it. Doug admired and respected his crew for their ingenuity and esprit de corps. He felt very proud of them and enjoyed watching their youthfulness.

"Vinnie! Goddamn it! Did you disconnect the governor?" Doug growled over the intercom.

Vinnie winced. "No, Sarge, Bailey did it."

"Vinnie, you lowlife little rat. Sarge, it was Vinnie's idea. He said if I didn't do it, he would."

"No, I didn't, sarge."

Pure pandemonium kicked off over the intercom among the three. Doug couldn't hold a straight face any longer and laughed hysterically. The others realized they'd fallen for Doug's fake anger, slowly caught the humor, and joined in. It turned into fleeting laughter. Looking skyward, Doug saw the sky had gradually filled with more small, puffy cumulus clouds showing a thunderstorm formation.

"We've been on the road for nearly forty minutes. It's time for a pit stop," Boz announced.

Vinnie keyed the mike and asked, "Hey, sarge, I know of a gas station ahead. I need a soda, too, and to use the can."

"Yeah, sarge, let's stop; I need a soda, too," Bailey chimed in. "Okay. By the way, I thought you said this turnoff was in only a few miles," Doug replied.

"The turnoff is less than five miles past the gas station. I'm sure," Vinnie assured him.

Vinnie saw the station about a quarter of a mile further up the road. The garage's south side had an old, wooden-framed shack attached to it, which served as a bar and grill restaurant with log siding. The gas station's only two pumps protruded vertically from a cement island under a small overhead cover made of corrugated steel.

A large gravel parking lot sat at the front and south side of the building for truckers and their rigs. On this day, the bar and grill were devoid of any patrons. Vinnie attributed this absence to fifteen outlaw biker motorcyclists, most likely with their girlfriends. They had filled up the bar and grill early on and probably got drunk and ate fast food. Any savvy motorist who stopped by would probably have gotten gas and departed quickly.

The bikers had ceremoniously parked their rides outside along the restaurant's front wall, which mainly contained picture windows. It gave patrons an unobstructed view of the majestic mountains. Today, however, the manager kept the curtains drawn to keep the bikers from looking outside and spotting an unsuspecting pigeon to pick on.

Vinnie pulled the tank into the parking lot and parked it on the east side of the restaurant, in a park-like, grassy enclosure, out of everyone's view so they wouldn't notice the tank.

Doug said, "Boz, you and Bailey go in first and get what you need, then Vinnie and I will go in."

Bailey and Boz climbed out of their hatches and descended from the side of the tank.

Doug called after them, "Don't take all year; get what you need and get back! I don't want to linger around here any longer than necessary and take a chance of getting spotted."

"Aye, aye, Skipper," Bailey piped back.

Since they had time, Vinnie related the story behind this place to Doug. An old man named Jenkins had claimed sole ownership of the gas station and the bar and grill. Jenkins came across like an old mountain goat hermit. He looked like a frail old man dressed in Levi coveralls and cowboy boots and wore an old, oil-soaked baseball cap with a big Cubs logo.

Old Man Jenkins prospered as a federally protected client in the witness protection program. His real name was Mario Colombo, and he had once worked with a bagman for the mob after making his "bones." Mario had changed his name to Todd Jenkins. He had received this property with the gas station for his cooperation and safety.

It turned out to be what he needed. Very old now, in his late seventies, Jenkins . . . for the first time in his life . . . felt some contentment. Jenkins, who was not a man to trifle with, hated authority . . . and that included cops and anyone else who wore a uniform. He didn't encourage their patronage on his property. Jenkins had already established himself with the bikers when he killed the two who tried to rob him one day.

He killed the third one when the biker tried to ambush him for killing his brother. Still a capable button man, Jenkins maintained his edge, even in his seventies. The bikers and Mr. Jenkins had negotiated and agreed.

Jenkins wouldn't kill the bikers if they visited the bar and grill on Saturdays, provided they paid their bill and didn't destroy the place. Jenkins promised to make sure no one disturbed them while they partied. Vinnie surmised that, on this day, the bikers had started early.

"How do you know all that?" Doug inquired suspiciously.

"Word gets around," Vinnie replied nonchalantly. Bailey walked to the old shack where Jenkins came from and saw him walk to his favorite chair and sit outside the door with his trademark pipe dangling from this old, wrinkled mouth.

"Good morning," Bailey chirped. "Do you have any soda pop in here?"

"No. It's over in the gift shop," Jenkins said in an icy tone as he pointed and nodded toward the restaurant.

"Where's the black dude going?"

"He's going to get a soda," Bailey said, walking away.

W.C. Hatounian

Bailey got a sick feeling. He'd seen the motorcycles like everyone else had when they pulled into the parking lot at the front of the bar and grill. They'd figured the bikers came for lunch. Boz walked in the door and disappeared from Bailey's view.

The builder had been innovative in constructing a small alcove inside the entrance, midway along the front wall, for easy access that wouldn't disturb the restaurant guests. He went to the bar's cash register, on the far right side of the bar, next to the restrooms and gift shop, and asked to buy some takeout burgers and fries.

The bartender was tending the bar and the register at the gift shop. He also served as a bouncer at night when they had a band and carried a girth the size of a haystack. While waiting for the bartender, Boz overheard him tell one of the biker patrons how he got this job.

The bartender had fallen into good fortune when old man Jenkins hired him right after being released from prison. He'd been on his way west and had stopped here for gas. Jenkins saw the tattoos and suspected a con, so he inquired into his past.

The haystack, not in any mood for questions, had felt annoyed by the question until Jenkins offered him a job. The haystack immediately changed his attitude, and he has stayed on ever since. He'd seen Jenkins in action and would not cross him. He eventually learned about Jenkins's experience as a Chicago button man.

Jenkins told the haystack he trusted no one who hadn't done time. He also assured the man that he'd share his bed with a dead fish if he attempted to cheat or rob him. The bartender understood and felt very grateful for a good job and a place to live, especially after seeing the old

54

man take out the three bikers.

The two lived in separate bungalows behind the property. Neither Jenkins nor the haystack ever had to leave the area if he didn't want to. For obvious reasons, the state troopers and county sheriff's officers did not frequent Jenkins' place.

"We don't serve servicemen here," the haystack boomed, looking over at Boz.

Boz immediately felt he had come into a place he should have avoided. A husky biker walked out of the men's room. He stood about six foot three and built like an ox without a neck. This bald biker wore a large tattoo with the letters AB on the upper-right tree trunk of a bicep.

He wore a cut-off Levi's jacket over a black T-shirt. With no one having to tell him, Boz figured AB didn't stand for Angel Baby. The biker looked at Boz with the coldest, meanest, hollow blue-gray eyes Boz had ever seen on a man's face.

"What you doin' in here, boy?" He growled.

Bailey entered the building and immediately sensed that big trouble was brewing.

"C'mon, Boz, time to go," Bailey said, tapping his left biceps with the back of his right hand.

"Boz?" the biker yelled. "That stand for bozo, eh, boy?"

The biker and the bartender laughed. Bailey winced and grabbed Boz's arm, and they both turned to leave without saying a word. The biker looked at Bailey and said, "Oh, look, the gook's tryin' to save his buddy."

The activity at the gift shop had attracted the attention of a few more bikers. Instinctively, Bailey and Boz both knew it was time to leave now.

The two moved toward the door, but three very mean-looking bikers blocked the exit.

"Look, fellas, we just want to leave," Bailey asserted.

"Yeah, we don't need any trouble," Boz added.

"No one asked you for a comment, boy," the tall biker by the door said menacingly.

Then, a large hand grabbed Boz by the right shoulder and spun him around. A giant fist greeted Boz's face from the bald biker. Because Boz instinctively moved his head at the last second, the punch landed right at the front of Boz's left ear, in line with his cheekbone. Boz went flying backward toward the wall and hit the floor.

"Look at bozo boy fly," the bald biker boomed. The rest of them broke into grave laughter. Bailey quickly moved to help Boz. One biker by the door kicked Bailey in the side and sent him crashing against the gift shop counter.

Doug felt Boz and Bailey were taking too long, and his worry meter pegged. He thought he heard some noise from inside the restaurant, but he wasn't sure. He went in and checked on them. Doug, fearing the worst, hurriedly opened the door to the restaurant. The two bikers who guarded the exit were leaning on the door and lost their balance, falling outside backward.

"Hey, look, another one!" One of them yelled as he took a swing at Doug.

Doug, a follower of Korean Tae-Kwan-do . . . which he'd learned from a Korean master he'd met in Vietnam . . . blocked the punch and broke the man's arm against the door with one swift move. Then he turned and drop-kicked the other biker. The remaining bikers turned their attention to Doug.

"Wakefield! Gunn! Get back to the vehicle," Doug ordered loudly.

As Angela often accused him of running out of patience, Vinnie couldn't stand waiting on the seat inside the cupola's hatch much longer before seeing about the commotion. As Vinnie approached the corner of the building, he saw old man Jenkins coming toward him with his shotgun cradled in his arms.

Vinnie decided it was better for him inside the tank than outside and returned to it, changing from worried to frantic. He didn't know what to do. Out of fear, he grabbed one of the .50-caliber ammunition boxes and loaded the machinegun in the cupola.

Since the tank still had full power, he thought he'd drive it around to the front of the building. Boz and Bailey attempted to make for the door when another biker tripped them.

"You two ain't going no place," he said.

"Look, we didn't come here looking for trouble. We're leaving," Doug said.

"Too late, sucker. You broke my friend's arm, and you'll pay for that."

"He was attempting to punch me," Doug replied.

"That ain't the way we see it," the big bald biker growled.

"Yeah," the choir of bikers chimed.

The biker with the broken arm crawled back inside and was quickly carried off by two friends. The rest of the group crowded into the gift shop area. Bailey turned to Boz and quietly said, "When I tell you, go for the door."

When the bald biker opened his mouth to speak, Bailey whispered, "Now!" And they both bolted for the door.

Doug stepped aside, let them through, and then stood in the doorway to block it.

"Man, you suckers are gonna eat shit now," the tall biker said, as he went for Doug.

Doug side-kicked the biker backward into his friends, then turned to get outside the building and run back to the tank. He guessed the boys were already aboard, and Vinnie would be ready to drive off. Ten feet outside the bar, Doug met old man Jenkins holding a double-barreled shotgun right at his guts.

"Stay where you are," Jenkins said.

When Bailey and Boz returned to Vicky and climbed aboard the tank, they saw Vinnie pointing the .50 toward the restaurant.

"Vinnie, what the hell you doin'?" Bailey questioned, out of breath.

"Covering Doug," Vinnie said, deadly serious and without emotion.

"Vinnie, you can't even see Doug. Besides, you can't just shoot those people with that thing, no matter how bad we want to do it," Bailey insisted.

"Christ, Vinnie, what did you do, load the fifty?" Boz asked, shocked.

"Bailey, get in the goddamn tank! Now they got Doug," Boz yelled. "Vinnie, get in your hole and do exactly as I say."

Boz had never in his life felt the anger he felt now. No one had ever provoked the hatred he experienced at this moment. No one had ever hit him with a sucker punch during the years he took boxing in high school and competed in college.

Boz never worried about defending himself, but he knew no one who wanted to kill him like these people of the Aryan Brotherhood. Boz got into the TC's hatch. Vinnie sat in the driver's seat and got ready to go. The crew put their helmets on and turned the selector switch on the intercom. Boz checked the sights of the .50.

"Okay, Vinnie, drive Vicky around to the front door. Let's get Doug out of there."

By this time, the bikers had emptied the bar. They felt the need for blood and tried to beat each other to Doug, who Jenkins held at gunpoint. Jenkins told the bikers to settle down; he'd let them have their fun in a minute.

The ground trembled like an earthquake as the noise of a loud, angry machine filled their ears. Everyone's heads turned when they heard Vicky's tracks clanking around the corner of the restaurant building.

Vinnie took a deliberately wide turn and aimed straight for the motorcycles, all nicely parked in a row. Bailey turned the turret slightly to the right and lowered the main gun to chest height for effect and for Doug to grab. The color in old man Jenkins's face drained to his feet, and he defecated in his pants.

He froze where he stood, his mouth agape and a death stare on his face. The shotgun slowly slipped from his bony, weak fingers and hit the ground. The bikers, surprised, immediately comprehended what had happened. They became horrified at the steel behemoth coming their way with a cannon the size of the Holland Tunnel.

They didn't even notice Doug push Jenkins aside and grab for the side of the tank to his right. She rolled to the front door and over every parked motorcycle, crushing them flat like beer cans. Boz turned the .50 and aimed it at the bikers. They unceremoniously fell over each other, trying to get inside the front door and out of sight of that .50-caliber machinegun.

When Doug had finally climbed aboard, Vinnie opened the throttle and made a hard left to avoid the gas pumps. Doing so caused the right rear corner of Vicky's track and drive sprocket to rip an eight-foot section of the building wall. Boz dropped inside, allowing Doug to get into the TC hatch.

Vinnie headed for the highway and turned north with the throttle wide open. The sky darkened to where it looked like dusk. A breeze blew hard enough to convulse the limbs of every tree violently, and the smell of rain hung in the wind, and the smell of rain hung in the wind. Doug felt the chill in the air, and a disconcerting feeling swept over him.

'Chapter VII

Vinnie saw the turnoff marked only by a small, decayed wooden sign-off to the right of the road. It read, "Road Closed to All But Local Traffic" . . . as if anyone lived this way. He figured it probably pertained to military vehicles only.

"Hey, sarge, there's the turnoff sign," Vinnie proclaimed. A sense of relief swept over Doug. Their drive took them nearer to the fort and away from the bikers, the damage they had caused during the skirmish, and the trouble he felt they were in for it.

Talking among themselves, Jenkins and the patrons left behind at his place soon accepted the pointlessness of calling the authorities. They considered old Man Jenkins an unpleasant character because of his attitude toward the police. The brawl had occurred on his property; they figured it was doubtful if the cops would even investigate.

Also, Jenkins imagined explaining to a police officer an army tank had come by from nowhere, squashed all those poor bikers' scooters, and then tore out half of a wall for no reason. He knew a statement like that alone after the cops stopped laughing would give any investigator a great deal of skepticism. A few miles after the turnoff, Doug told Vinnie to pull over.

He told the men to take a short pit stop, drink water, and open a case of Meals Ready to Eat or MREs to satisfy their hunger. A mild dizziness slowly crept over Doug as they continued, but he didn't give it much thought or say anything. They'd traveled on the turnoff for about fifteen minutes, cruising at a comfortable forty miles per hour.

"How much farther to the gate?" Doug asked of everyone.

"I don't know, sarge, but it can't be far. Besides, we're still on schedule. According to my calculations, we must assume the company is still on the north-south road, and we should intercept them as planned," Vinnie answered.

"I'll check the map, sarge, and tell ya in a minute," Boz offered.

"How's your face, Boz?" Doug inquired.

"It's okay; Bailey put some cream on it from his first aid kit that seems to work," Boz replied.

"Bailey! How's your side?"

"I'm okay, sarge."

"Looks like about eight to ten klicks to the military reservation boundary," Boz concluded.

"Okay, that should put us on the mark," Doug thought aloud. He then added,

"Hey, I didn't see the rail line, or any abandoned buildings you said paralleled this road."

"They're farther down this way," Vinnie offered. Suddenly, an enormous thunderclap erupted and jolted everyone. Vinnie took his foot off the pedal and slowed the tank. He'd already turned on the headlights from the lighting control switch on the driver's master control panel, and he drove cautiously.

Again, another thunderclap sounded over their heads, followed by another. It reminded Doug of incoming rounds of artillery and the failed ambush in Vietnam. Almost instantly and without warning, sheets of rain poured on them from the blackened sky.

"Button up!" Doug commanded, and the crew quickly closed the hatches.

They rode inside in the humidity and discomfort. The vents remained open to let in air, which felt good on their worn and tired faces. It felt like the day was already over, and they should have made camp and been resting in their tents, not riding around back roads, but actually, it was only 12:10 p.m.

The dirt road ahead dissolved in the fog in front of Vinnie's face. He slowed Vicky more because of the poor visibility. He also slowed his pace while he looked through his commander's periscope simultaneously as Boz looked through his gunner's control periscope.

"Christ, Vinnie, how can you see?" Boz asked.

"I can't," Vinnie replied. "I'm turning on the brights."

"Take it as slow as you have to, Vinnie. We want to be safe and sound, even if we're late. Besides, I'm sure the rest of the company is getting drenched, too."

Doug offered, feeling confident they were getting nearer to the rest of the company. Peering out of the cupola, Doug watched the lightning turn into something that looked like nothing he'd ever seen. It danced in waves like a piano player's fingers moving across a keyboard. The peculiar thing was that the thunder did not stay in sync with the lightning, as it usually does in a thunderstorm.

Lightning usually comes first, and then thunder, in a one-two rhythm . . . but today, the thunder came erratically, sometimes before the lightning or not. The lightning sometimes made a spiderweb pattern in the sky and danced like lightning in a Frankenstein movie. The rain hit so hard that it blurred the road ahead of the headlights.

"Sarge, I can't see the road anymore. I'm gonna have to stop," Vinnie stated.

"Okay, we'll look for a place to pull off. Boz, use the thermal sights and see if there's a spot we can pull off this road," Doug ordered.

Vinnie turned on the night vision switch on his driver's master control panel while Boz turned on the tank thermal sight control switch or TTS. Boz increased the magnification to maximum and swept the turret back and forth across the road, looking for open space.

"Hey, I see a spot. It looks like an old shack or hut."

"Where?" Doug asked.

"About twenty meters to the right front."

"Okay, you see it yet, Vinnie?" Doug asked.

"Yeah, I think so," Vinnie replied.

"Boz, swing the main gun around so Vinnie can see better," Doug ordered.

Vinnie tried to focus on the old hut when they got closer to the spot. It sat in a clearing with a tree line behind and to the far left side. He pulled off the road, drove to the hut's right side, and then looked for a dry spot behind it.

He turned left and pulled the tank parallel to the opposite side of the hut under a row of large maple trees that made a natural carport, providing some protection from the rain.

"Let's leave our gear here and just take our ponchos and flashlights," Doug suggested.

The men took off their coveralls and grabbed their ponchos. Doug got the flashlights. He knew the ponchos should keep them dry and warm for a little while. After Vinnie shut Vicky down, they climbed out of the tank, secured the hatches, and made for the hut.

Doug noticed the hut's construction comprised mud and straw and had a grass roof. There was only a dirt floor on the inside. More grass cuttings and piles of straw heaped in the corners looked like someone had stored them there. The roof leaked slightly, but not severely enough to make the place uninhabitable.

Each of the three walls had a window space cut out in the center.

The wall with the door space faced the road, allowing some rain to get inside. A wooden frame for a door might have existed there at one time. The wall next to the tank seemed the driest, with an enormous pile of straw piled against it.

The men each found a spot and sat down. Doug thought they probably wondered how long it would be before getting underway again.

"This place reminds me of one of those huts from medieval England, like in Sherwood Forest," Bailey said.

Everyone chuckled.

"Yeah, and I bet an old witch lived here, too," Vinnie said.

"Yeah, Vinnie, you were born cursed by witches," Boz responded.

"No, by two sisters, but just as bad," Vinnie added.

The rumbling of the clouds took on a rhythmic tone.

Doug told his crew, "Settle into a comfortable position within the straw, everyone, and get some rest."

Whoa, what's going on? I'm feeling a bizarre, hypnotic effect. Listening to and transfixed by the weather outside's harmonic rhythm, a feeling of extreme fatigue crept over Doug. It sapped his ability to focus on where he was. A peculiar odor in the damp air seemed to emanate from the straw.

After they instinctively crawled into their ponchos, each man fell into a deep slumber and dreamed of nothing, their minds devoid of cognition or feeling. Outside, the storm raged with the power and vengeance of a typhoon. A lightning storm emerged again and danced its bony, macabre fingers along the tree line, exploding branches with a barrage of strikes.

A shower of branches and leaves tumbled from the sky and covered Vicky, obscuring her. In the far distance and unknown to the sleeping tank crew, an awful howling roar that would have terrified anyone who'd heard it defiled the sky.

Doug possessed no frame of reference to gauge how long they'd slept. It did not feel like he'd been asleep, but more like he'd been slipped a sedative. His mind slowly responded to reality. He opened his eyes to see a new morning and a clear sky out of the window hole. The rain had stopped, and it felt strangely warm. Doug immediately felt the discomfort of heavy humidity hanging in the air, leftover from the storm.

He heard birds singing in the trees, and the weather seemed very peaceful. Bailey felt a cold steel blade tapping across his neck, and someone else kicked his foot. As he slowly regained consciousness, his brain still in a damp fog, he heard someone speaking to him.

"Awake … awake, knave! Awake, I say."

Bailey opened his eyes and became startled to see four large men with long, broad swords, dressed in chain mail and wearing iron helmets. They each carried a shield with a unique design or crest. Bailey reached over and shook Vinnie, who sat upright with a start.

"Wa' . . was . . what is it?" He said, rubbing his eyes and trying to adjust to the abnormal situation. One of the other strangers prodded Boz and Doug.

"Oh crap, it's daylight," Vinnie said in a panic.

"It seems we've overslept, so we'd better get going. We're going to have a lot of explaining to do," Doug announced as he stood and brushed the pieces of straw off himself, not taking full cognizance of the other occupants in the room.

The rest of the crew finally got themselves off the floor and dismissed the strangers and their odd dress. When Doug attempted to move, one stranger poked him in the stomach with his sword and said, "And where dost thou think thou art going, knave?"

Who the hell are these characters?

"Look, whoever you are, we don't have the time to play games this morning. We have to get on the road. You guys in some show?" Doug asked sternly.

"Ouch, quit prodding me with your sword, tin man," Bailey chimed.

"Hey, from where did you come? I thought the amusement park around here closed years ago," Vinnie said. "Whatever you're trying to sell, we're not interested."

"Either we've gone to wonderland, or my deck of cards has just come alive," Boz replied.

"Enough," bellowed the oldest knight, dressed in a black and red suit of armor with a checker pattern and sporting a rotund figure with a lot of gray hair in his beard. He looked like the King of diamonds.

"Into the cart with them," the knight ordered soldiers outside.

Four more men, not dressed in ornate uniforms and who looked like soldiers, entered the hut and took Bailey and Vinnie by the arms.

"Hey, let go," Vinnie demanded, struggling.

Bailey attempted to resist one of the armed men when Boz grabbed the man and pushed him off Bailey. The strangers took a fighting stance with their swords. The crewmen got concerned and backed against a wall. Doug decided something was wrong with this picture and quickly asked, "Who exactly are you people, and what do you want with us?"

The rotund stranger stepped forward and said, "We are the knights from the Castle Darpon, in quest of runaway young women of age."

"Do we look like women?" Doug responded.

"Nay, but ye wouldst make good slaves."

"We are free-born men who have done no wrong," Doug replied.

"Aye, but ye art strangers, and we have not seen of you afore," suggested the youngest knight, dressed in a blue and white striped suit of armor.

"Look, Ace, we have never heard of any castles in this area, so if you're playing some game, we're not interested. We have to get to the Fort . ."

"Game? What game?" interrupted the older knight, who was the apparent leader.

"You guys are putting us on, and we don't have the time for it. We're not interested if you're in some carnival, which is a promotional ploy. So please allow us to leave, or there will be grave consequences," Doug spoke with finality.

"Enough of this banter. Take these men to the cart. The King will decide their fate," the old knight said. "And, if ye strange men resist, we will run you through here and now."

"Okay, fellas, let's get outside," Doug suggested to his crewmen.

The soldiers again seized the crewmen and took them outside and away from the hut. Doug noticed four more soldiers mounted on horseback and armed with crossbows guarding an ox cart with a cage mounted on it. When Doug tried to get his bearings, he quickly realized that the countryside had drastically changed.

The two-lane, desert-like dirt road he remembered being here transformed into a narrow trail. Sometimes, the shrubs and trees were sparser, denser, and taller than others. The lush forest that had been a desert beckoned them.

"Hey, sarge, are we just going to let them take us without a fight?" Vinnie questioned.

"This is bullshit, sarge," Boz added.

"Yeah, I know, but something is wrong here, and it isn't just with these people."

"What do you mean, sarge?" Bailey inquired.

"Just look around you; it's not the same."

One soldier came up to the group and said, "It's a long trip to the castle, so if ye need to use yonder tree, ye better make good use of it. There'll be no stopping," pointing toward a large evergreen tree with a nod of his head. Another large tree to the side of the hut still obscured Vicky.

"Good idea; we ought to take care of business while we can," Doug said.

The crewmen walked to the large tree and relieved themselves under the watchful eye of the soldiers.

"Can you see Vicky?" Boz asked Vinnie under his breath.

"Yeah, I can. She's hidden under the debris. Just look under the lowest fallen tree branches, and you can see her tracks," Vinnie whispered excitedly.

"Good. At least we know Vicky is still with us," Doug added.

"Since they're so intent on finding women, I'd like to give them a taste of Vicky's finer assets," Vinnie whispered.

"Yeah, a lot of good that does us; if we try to make a break for it, those goons with the crossbows will cut us down," Bailey said.

"I feel like these characters aren't fooling around; only I can't figure out what they're up to," Boz said.

"I don't know about this, but I can ask them," Doug replied.

"What are you planning on doing, sarge?" Bailey inquired.

"I'm simply going to ask them what's going on," Doug answered and proceeded to where the rotund knight stood with the other three knights.

Before Doug reached the knights, two soldiers grabbed him. "And where do ye think ye are going?" Asked one of them.

"I was going to ask the good knights a few questions," Doug responded.

"Prisoners may not speak to a knight without permission," the other soldier holding Doug responded.

"Well, can I speak?"

"No. Get ye into the cart, the lot of ya," ordered the soldier.

The other soldiers moved and prodded the crewmen toward the cart. It had only a two-wheeled single-axle platform, a wooden floor, wooden rails, and a gate for hauling small livestock . . . and prisoners.

"This is kidnapping, sarge," Vinnie protested.

"Yes, I know, Vinnie, but these characters are serious, so let's do what they tell us until we find out what's happening. Just take it one step at a time."

While the crewmen got into the cart, Vinnie turned to one soldier and asked,

"Hey, Jack o' Hearts, what are you looking for unmarried young women for anyhow?"

"The harvest festival is upon us, and they will be anxious."

"Who are they . . . your pet dragons?"

Vinnie saw the most controlled look of terror he'd ever seen on a human face. The rest of the men had heard Vinnie's quip and saw the soldier's expression. The soldier turned pale; beads of perspiration formed on his face, and his eyes seemed to have recessed into his skull with a broad and wild look.

His lips stretched across his teeth as if he were in agony, and the bony features of his gaunt face protruded. The man was terrified. Each soldier took to their steed and mounted it. Although the men became cramped inside the cart, Doug intended to take advantage of speaking in hushed tones without easily being heard by the soldiers.

When the cart moved away, Vinnie thought he heard a faint metallic whine coming from Vicky's direction.

"Hear that?" Vinnie asked.

"What?" Bailey responded.

"It came from over there where Vicky's hidden." He motioned with his chin.

"No, Vinnie, I heard nothing; you're just getting spooked after talking to that soldier."

"Hey, sarge, why do you suppose that soldier freaked out when I used the word 'dragon'? You don't think there are any actual dragons around here, do ya?" Vinnie asked.

"All right, let's settle down. No, Vinnie, I don't. Those were only myths, so forget it," Doug ordered.

"Okay, sarge, you're the history expert."

"What do you make of this?" Boz asked.

"Take a moment to look around and see these people dressed in nine-hundred-year-old clothing, weapons, and armor. The area doesn't look like Colorado. We're sitting in an actual ox cart, pulled by a real ox, which is no stage prop, as you can tell if you look under this straw and see the dried animal dung under it.

"It takes a long time to accumulate that much buildup. Those men's facial features don't even look like today's people. We've seen people who look like a Neanderthal now and then, but that's the exception rather than the rule.

"The craftsmanship of their clothing, weapons, and this cart shows they are not twentieth-century copies. No, fellas, something has changed."

"You trying to say we somehow . . . we're not in 1991 anymore . . . we've gone back in time?" Boz gulped.

"Well, men, we have to draw our conclusions. I'm no expert in the space-time continuum business, but I can safely speculate. I don't think we're in Kansas anymore, as the saying goes," Doug replied.

"Okay, what do we do?" Bailey inquired.

"We have to make every attempt to escape at the first opportunity we get. Either all of us or one of us has to get back to Vicky. Then we can deal with these people and whatever is going on from a, shall we say, stronger position," Doug answered. "Stay alert and make mental notes. Watch where we're going and memorize landmarks."

"Yes, we ought to be taking in the countryside and figuring out how far we're traveling, so we know how to get back," Boz agreed.

"Boz's right. We need to keep our bearings at all times. Boz, you calculate the mileage. Vinnie, you keep a log of compass headings. You have your compass, don't you? Bailey and I will note landmarks, troop strengths, and population. We will need a sound plan for escape and evasion," Doug said.

"Yeah, sarge, I've got my compass and my Swiss Army knife; never leave home without them. How about you guys?"

They nodded, indicating they had similar equipment.

W.C. Hatounian

"Where's your flashlight, Vinnie?" Doug asked.

"Still in my BDU cargo pocket, sarge," Vinnie replied, grinning.

´Chapter VIII

As the crewmen continued along the road with the convoy of knights and soldiers, Doug noted they entered a large, dense, green forest. The men took mental notes on distances, headings and landmarks.

The guards had not searched them before placing them into the cart. Doug felt confident they would keep possession of the items in their pockets and their GI wristwatches. The men hid those items under the long sleeves of their battle dress uniforms.

"Boz, how long have we been on the road?" Doug asked.

"About an hour, sarge."

"Okay, men. I want you to take a mental inventory of the contents of your pockets without taking them out and letting the soldiers see."

"What's this . . . Sherwood Forest?" Boz questioned.

"Yeah, maybe we'll get saved by Robin Hood!" Vinnie quipped, and the men chuckled.

Doug turned around and got on his knees. He motioned to one soldier riding nearby and came over to Doug.

"Hey, how much farther is it to this castle?" He asked.

"We'll be there afore supper time," replied the soldier.

"Is it a common practice to take people captive for no reason?"

"We know not of ye, and all strangers are suspect. We have peace now, and nothing must disturb it."

"But we were just passing through and meant no harm to your people . . ."

Then, one knight, who looked like the King of clubs and wore black-and-white, flower-patterned armor, rode over and dismissed the soldier.

"Stop your chatter with this soldier," the knight said gruffly.

"Pardon me, my lord, but I was merely inquiring about the meaning of this outrage. We are freeborn men who have disturbed no one's peace here and are just passing through your realm. Is that a crime?" Doug asked.

"If that were true, why are ye dressed strangely, like a bush? Is it that thou might travel through our land and not see and disturb the peace by awakening their anger? Oh, pray tell, we have had many a stranger who has come saying he was merely passing through and on a quest for truth. They would hide their armor and horse until they sought them out and found them.

"It took many a year and a powerful king to enforce the peace. Every door and tree had a royal proclamation hanging, forbidding any quests in our kingdom. Even so, they came. Later, when enough of those who came to do battle had not prevailed and thus devoured, the King decided to seize anyone who entered this land and required them to prove they were not in disguise. This way, we save a foolish man's life and preserve the peace," the knight proclaimed.

"My lord, I speak the truth. We are not on any quest. What need we do to prove our intent?"

"Christ, sarge!" Bailey mumbled to Doug. "This sounds like a Shakespeare play."

"It is not for me to decide. The King will see your truth or falsehood," the knight boomed.

"What is the penalty for those who have lied to the King?" Doug inquired.

"The rope or the fire, depending on one's status," the King of clubs replied.

"You would allow a true knight to die without honor at the end of a rope? I find that inexcusable," Doug needled.

By the disgusted look on the knight's face, he did not favor the penalty when applied to other knights who naturally did what they expected.

However, the King's word was law, and no code of knighthood, vow, oath, or amount of pleading had come remotely close to changing the King's mind. The knight didn't appreciate the ugly suggestion from a stranger. In his opinion, the King didn't even seem near the knight's requirements or caliber, causing his indignation to worsen.

"Enough!" the knight bellowed, and then he rode off.

"So, they think we're on a quest. Well, that cuts it. When the King gets a load of us, it's the stake," Bailey offered.

"What quest is he talking about, sarge?" Vinnie asked.

W.C. Hatounian

"Well, in the olden days, when knighthood was popular, these guys expected to find a quest . . like the Crusades, for example, and prove themselves or compete among themselves. Back then, they had a purpose for living. . . kind of like drag racing when I was a kid."

"Or like jousting," Bailey added.

"Yeah, I'd like to bring Vicky to one of those jousting matches. Get on one end of the field, lower her 105-millimeter gun in the jousting position, and tell the knights: joust this, Tin Man!" Vinnie remarked.

Vinnie's comment put everyone's feelings into perspective. Doug saw the effect that the long voyage through the thick forest was having on the men; although uneventful, it was still causing a lot of anticipation. The men had a difficult time trying to memorize the landmarks.

The trip often got bumpy and dusty, and they plodded along. Everyone felt tired and very uncomfortable, crammed in the small cart. When the cart finally broke out of the heavy forest and crested a steep hill, Doug discreetly checked his wristwatch, which read 5:00 p.m.

A castle and its surrounding grounds lie below in the center of a lush green valley. Doug estimated the valley stretched about eight to ten miles long and was about the same distance wide. He noticed the castle did not have a moat, but it had battlements and four towers.

Doug felt this was the most beautiful, picturesque valley he'd ever seen, and he understood why the ruler intended to keep the peace at any price . . . but against what? Who were they or them? Perhaps a warrior class of people lived on the outskirts of the Kingdom in the high hills. It surrounded the valley and posed no harm unless attacked by every knight who passed by and wished to make a name for himself.

Yes, that's it! It's the only logical answer, Doug guessed. The King blessed the peace by giving his counterpart a few nice, new, unmarried young girlfriends for his harem every year. That explained the look of terror on the soldier's face. If they didn't maintain the peace, the penalty was akin to getting orders to the Russian front in World War II.

Doug shared his theory with the rest of the crew, and they agreed it must be the answer . . . all except Vinnie. Vinnie felt something more going on here than the wild tribesmen theory, except he didn't know what.

Chapter IX

The procession exited from the forest. Doug could see a treelined dirt road that intersected the one they were on and eventually led to the castle from the higher ground. While watching the slowly setting sun, he kept rolling over escape scenarios in his mind. As they strolled along slowly, Doug pointed out to the crewmen that the fields on both sides of the road have filled with growing wheat, corn, barley, alfalfa, and other vegetation.

Far beyond the fields, he saw hills and lush tree lines indicative of forested areas. He saw peasants tilling the crops, cattle and horses littering the open, grassy fields. Feeling cramped and tired, Doug was grateful when the gaggle of knights, soldiers, and prisoners finally arrived at the castle complex.

"I guess we're here," Bailey said in a low, speculative voice.

"Geez, look at this place," Vinnie said, stunned.

"Looks like a blooming Camelot, doesn't it?" Boz added, affecting a

British accent.

The castle grounds transfixed Doug. The procession turned right onto the main wide boulevard leading directly to the front of the castle. He saw an abundant, thick, green grass lawn filled in on both sides. It sat within meticulously manicured flowerbeds alongside the road and across the front of the castle's entrance, bordered by low hedges.

Instead of the expected drawbridge, a circular cobblestone driveway led to the main entrance. It looped back around to the main roadway. An ornate bronze water fountain in the center of the circle depicted wood nymphs in various forms of dance around an obelisk. Two sweeping staircases descending from the opposite sides of the main doors paralleled the circular driveway. They went up to a broad, balcony-like structure, which continued around the concave front wall halves.

The doors opened upon the sergeant of the guard announcing the royal knights and their party. The procession turned into the main driveway of the entrance and proceeded along a wide thoroughfare. Cobblestone streets within the castle grounds provided accessible transit through the marketplaces and interior buildings. Doug noticed too many things, apparently out of place. It seemed inaccurate for the period he was trying to define in his mind.

"Sarge, I'm no history expert like you, but what period is this?" Vinnie wondered out loud.

"It looks like it's a clash of eras. Notice we're inside a medieval castle with French provincial walls. Adorned with English Tudor fascia, the buildings inside the walls and window treatments accented the confusion of eras. Manicured gardens with feudal-looking people working the...

I don't know, Vinnie. It's a mystery to me, too," Doug answered.

"Look at the sentries . . . they're dressed in Napoleonic uniforms and armed with lances and sabers. Nothing fits this era, sarge. This conflict of cultures does not seem to portray a very accurate picture, just an elaborately confusing one. It has become a bad dream, and slowly getting worse," Bailey concluded.

"Yeah, and they all speak English differently," Vinnie added.

Bailey and Boz pondered the dimensions of the fortifications. The castle seemed oriented east-west, with the rear-facing east. They observed a large tower toward the western corner of the castle, topped by a flat turret. The ramparts on top of the castle seemed unguarded. There weren't any guards around the interior grounds, either.

Doug sighed in relief when the cart stopped a few feet beyond an open intersection under an archway. He saw the four knights up ahead continue along the road to the north. As the soldiers dismounted, they allowed the prisoners to exit the cage. The men stretched their cramped arms and legs.

The guards quickly ushered Doug and the crew into a doorway and down a long, sweeping, spiral staircase of tan marble, in what seemed like a section of dungeons. A set of stairs led to an open area with six jail cell doors arranged in a semicircle.

The walls and floors looked like limestone material. Hallways led away from this first dungeon complex in two directions. Gaslights or oil lamps on the walls illuminated the passageways and dungeon area.

Doug noticed the jail guards wore brown tights made of heavy wool and quilted jackets, apparently to help them endure the cold and dampness. The room's center had a large, round wooden table with six wooden chairs for the guards.

One guard opened the center cell and gestured for the men to go inside. The spaciousness of the cell and the six bunk beds made of heavy timber impressed Doug. The floors were spotless. Two candle holders sat on a wooden, picnic-like table with bench seats in the center of the cell.

He examined the beds and found one straw mattress and one wool blanket on each level, with a "honey bucket" sitting on the side of each unit. The senior knight who led the search party went directly to the King's offices next to the throne room.

He knew the King was not on the second floor, which contained the King and queen's residences. The knight entered the King's outer office. The Louis XIV décor, including the curtains on the windows that overlooked the rear castle gardens, never impressed him.

The King's valet announced the knight and admitted him into the inner office. The King, Alexander I, sat behind his Louis XIV-style desk. He wore only his shirtsleeves and trousers in a casual manner. A tall, thin man in his thirties with a lean and pale face, the King sported graying, long, thin brown hair prematurely and wore a small goatee on his chin but was otherwise clean-shaven. His light brown eyes, indifferent but commanding, gave him the look of a psychopath.

"Well, Sir Dentworth, what news have thee?" The King commanded.

"We have taken four prisoners, Your Majesty. We found them a'hiding in the old witch's hut, not a half day's ride from here."

"What is their crime?"

"They have come on a quest. These men wear strange clothing . . . and I, fer one, would not believe their purpose here is not to destroy the peace."

"We shall see. I will hold court in one hour. Bring your prisoners, then."

"Aye, Your Majesty." Sir Dentworth bowed and withdrew from the King's offices.

"I guess this is it until our trial or something," Vinnie said.

"Yeah. But again, what would seem logical to us might not be logical to these people in this medieval period," Boz corrected him.

Vinnie saw a soldier come downstairs and hand the senior jail guard a message.

"It says to remove the prisoners and feed them," the guard said, looking confused.

"Well, what are you waiting for?" The soldier growled.

The guard removed his keys from the metal clip on his leather belt, opened the cell door, and motioned the men to step out. Doug and the crew followed the guard through the archway to their left and proceeded down the long hallway in front.

Doug observed that the walls and floor turned into a cut stone material along the hallway. In an alternating pattern between the left and right sides, torches mounted every twenty feet lighted the way. The hallway opened into a large room.

A large fireplace with a door to its right in the room's entrance, a stone staircase on the right, two doors on the left, and old tapestries hung throughout. Four guards ushered the men through the door next to the fireplace and came upon another group of four guards going in the other direction.

A guard motioned for them to go through an archway. The men found themselves in a dining room or a mess hall; the room appeared large enough to seat approximately fifty people. And furnished with wooden tables and benches to sit on. One table had food: fruit, greens, and meats served on platters. There was no silverware.

A server waved the men over to their table. Doug saw the guards sat at another table and were getting served by a scullery maid. Large goblets filled with what smelled like ale stood around a large brass pitcher on the crewmen's table.

Doug noticed only two other doors besides the one they had used to enter. One door faced them, centered on the far wall, and the other was on the adjacent wall to the right of that one.

"Do ya think we ought to eat this stuff, sarge?" Vinnie asked quietly.

"I think the fruit and the greens are all right, but I'd be real careful about the meat," Doug responded.

"Think they'd try to drug us?" Boz Inquired.

"No, I don't think they're that smart. Besides, it would take their fun away," Doug suggested.

The men slowly and cautiously ate the food using their hands.

"Beer tastes funny, sarge," Vinnie commented.

"It's ale, Vinnie. This ale is going to taste very different from our American beer. As for the rest of you, don't get drunk; we need to remain as sober as possible to get the hell out of here."

"Hey, sarge, the meat is pretty tasty, and it seems well done," announced Boz.

"Your call, men. If you're starving, eat as much as you can. We don't know if or when we'll eat again."

The men then ate their fill, knowing Doug was right. Without warning, the center door opened, and Sir Dentworth entered with six soldiers who looked like the palace guards, wearing the same Napoleonic-style uniforms.

"You men, come along," he ordered.

"Guess it's showtime," Doug said.

Dentworth led the guards and the men back to where they had entered the open room with the six jail cells. It continued along the opposite hallway for about ninety paces, counted by Vinnie. Doug noticed three small, separate open areas about twenty steps apart along this passageway. A door sat opposite a metal ladder on the wall, which they assumed likely led to the outside area.

When Doug and the men arrived at the base of a staircase, the guards prodded them to ascend it. At the top landing, the men went through a wooden door and down another hallway, only this one had glossy, tiled floors and paneled walls with portraits of knights and ladies. They then entered a large, ornate throne room through a side door.

Astounded at the setting, Doug recognized he was standing in a French eighteenth-century-style room. The floors, made of marble, had onyx and gold inlays. The papered walls held many gas lamps and paintings he did not recognize.

Chairs graced the walls for the ladies to sit; otherwise, the furniture was sparse except for three crystal chandeliers hanging from the ceiling. Doug expected to see Louis XIV himself at any minute.

On the highest portions of the main walls above the thrones were stained-glass windows on both sides. Dentworth turned left, brought the men into the throne room, rounded a corner, and continued a few feet.

The group reached the rear of the throne room, turned, and faced the front. The large, ornately carved throne room doors remained closed behind them. The white-painted room had gold trim and accents. The knight turned and bellowed, "Ye must wait here!" And then turned and walked toward the front of the room. Soon after, the doors opened, and the lords and ladies of the court entered. The multitude, eager to see the King dispense justice to foreigners who disrupted their way of life, rejoiced in anticipation of the coming entertainment.

After the strange men arrived, the King sent a crier to announce the special tribunal. He intended to hold court at 7:00 p.m. Doug could not get over the disparity among the people's attire entering the room. They dressed in clothing from various periods, from the sixteenth century to the eighteenth century.

The crowd, composed of men and women of varying sizes, shapes, and ages, fanned themselves in the warm air as they waited anxiously. For the first time, the crewmen saw the makeup of the castle's local population.

"Either this room needs more airing, or these people badly need a bath," Vinnie whispered.

Doug noticed the crowd ignored him and the rest of the men as if they didn't exist. Even though most of the room had an eighteenth-century European flavor, the décor surrounding the King's throne displayed a medieval appearance.

"Sarge, no one's even looking at us. Let's go," Bailey suggested.

"Good idea," Doug said. "But what do you recommend we do with the guard detail behind us?"

When the men casually looked behind them, they realized the knight wasn't so dumb. Besides the personal guard detail, there along the perimeter walls stood the King's household cavalry.

Doug saw the soldiers were taking in every move he and the crewmen made. The soldiers resembled ornately dressed Russian hussars in black uniforms with silver buttons and silver accents. They also wore black bearskin hats with silver chinstraps.

Unknown to everyone else, a contingent of the feared Red Guard, loyal only to the sorcerer Zenega, watched the prisoners with great interest from a hidden balcony above the throne room.

"We must pay these new people a visit and see who they are and what they want," the leader said to a subordinate sergeant, who nodded in approval.

"Christ, this place has no rhyme or reason," Doug said, disgusted.

"I guess we should stay for the party," Vinnie joked.

Without warning, a loud bang, bang, bang on the floor came from near the front of the throne. The people faced forward and remained bowed. The robed individual with the large staff to the left of the throne announced the King.

"Lords and Ladies, His Majesty, the King, Alexander the First, ruler of all Xanpathia."

The crewmen stood silently. Everyone except the soldiers bowed. The King entered from the right of the throne and seated himself. The throne platform, raised four steps high, had doors on each side hidden behind the curtains hanging from the ceiling.

King Alexander wore his royal crimson robes and a simple gold crown with four peaks in the shapes of fleurs-de-lis. Doug could see the crew's discomfort with the King's regal demeanor. In Doug's mind, he exemplified the King of spades. The people righted themselves and waited for the fun to start.

"Sir Dentworth," called the King.

"Aye, Yer Majesty," the knight replied with a bow.

"Where are your scavengers?" The King inquired in his soft, English tone, minus the medieval brogue.

The knight turned and put out his arm. As the people moved to the sides, the crewmen became exposed, and the two closest guards began prodding them with their lances. The four walked to the throne. Doug knew by the King's face that the cards had become stacked against them no matter what he said.

"And who might you people be?" The King asked calmly.

Doug took one step forward and said, "We are merely humble travelers, not of this land or time. We have inadvertently entered your kingdom without notice or reason and only wish to return to our place."

"Well, put. However, your appearance betrays you. A man of color, a man with strange eyes. . .humble travelers, indeed. Do you take me for a fool?"

"Of course not, Your Majesty," Doug replied.

"I, for one, have never seen this type of dress. It appears to be that of men who would conceal themselves from either thievery or evil. Like mercenaries who might attack an unsuspecting person and take his purse. . .or attack a group of soldiers without notice and easily defeat them. Are there more of you? Is this some form of sorcery?" The King demanded.

Doug thought quickly. The King had him cornered.

No matter what I answer, the King will not buy it. A bluff might work.

"Yes, Your Majesty, there are thousands more in a faraway land. They would never come here unless there is a threat against us."

"Your intentions here in my kingdom are not convincing to me. I believe you are mercenaries of some kind and here on your own. I am curious about how you arrived here."

"We were . . .ah, walking down the path when a heavy storm struck us, and we took shelter in a hut we found. Your soldiers woke us the next morning and brought us here."

"Is that true, Sir Dentworth?" Asked the King.

"Aye, Your Majesty."

"I do not discount your version of your arrival to our land. I am always suspicious of those who have come in disguise for a personal quest, thus causing a disturbance of the peace. I see no horses, no armor, no weapons. I find that very curious but disturbing. You will be my guests until I consult with Lord Zenega; then, I will decide what will become of you. Until then, do not attempt to escape. The penalty is death. Sir Dentworth, I leave them in your care."

King Alexander rose and left the way he had come. The people again humbled themselves until he had departed the room. The knight motioned for the guards to return the men to their cells.

The original four medieval guards took charge of the crewmen and led them back toward the staircase where they had come. The knight and his guard detail went in the opposite direction.

Doug observed he and the men had returned to the large dining room, passed through it to the opposite door, and then traveled down a flight of stairs to another door. It opened onto an extensive square area with eight barred doors, two on each wall leading to the guest rooms. An old, fat jailer sat at a table in the middle with a large key ring on his left side and a leather apron around his waist. The jailer rose and unlocked a cell.

"All right, in with ya." He motioned.

Doug saw the floor covered with straw and oil lamps hung on metal hooks on each side of the cell. Four wood-framed beds sat along each wall with straw-filled mattresses. The room looked large enough to hold twenty to thirty men. The wall opposite the door's barred window looked into a courtyard. This cell looked dark and dingy compared to the other one they'd seen.

When the guards left, Vinnie said, "Don't you love these guest quarters?"

"Yeah, real homey," Boz offered.

"Now I know what the Count of Monte Cristo felt like," Bailey said.

"C'mon, let's think of how to break the hell out of here," whispered Vinnie excitedly.

"Hold on a minute; I want to see if the jailer can provide some information," Doug said.

Doug walked to the cell door and looked through the bars. He saw the jailer reading something by lamplight. That's odd; the jailer is reading what looks like a book. This place is confusing me.

"Excuse me, but can I have a word with you?"

The jailer looked at Doug and formed a smile on his cherubic face. He looked like a family man or a farmer, not a jailer to Doug.

"What is it yer needing?" He asked.

"I'm sorry to disturb you, but we have come from a different place, and I was curious about life here in your land. I'd like to know about your ways."

"So what is it ye be wanting to know?" The jailer asked with a smile.

"Well, you don't look like a jailer."

"'Tis true, I'm not. I'm a blacksmith."

"Then why are you here?"

"Because I must forge the chains for yer hands and feet on the morrow. You men are the only prisoners here. We're not accustomed to having prisoners here, seeing as how everyone lives peacefully. Otherwise, yer hung or burned at the stake."

"Do you live here in the castle?"

"Nay, nay, I live in a village half-league from here."

"I didn't see a village when we arrived."

"That's because you came from the south road. The villages are to the north of the valley off this road."

"I did not see any abbeys or evidence of religious symbols anywhere. Can you explain that?"

The jailer looked puzzled.

"What is an abbey or a religious symbol?"

"Don't you people believe in a supreme being, a god . . . things like that?"

"We know of no such beliefs. All we have is the King."

"Where is this place, Xanpathia? Is it in Europe or what?"

"I know not what you mean. Xanpathia is in Xanpathia. It is our land."

"Has anyone ever left Xanpathia and returned?"

"Nay, never a man has left our land. For what purpose would he go?"

Even though Doug wasn't an investigator, he knew brainwashing when he heard it.

"The King said he would speak to a person called Zenega. Who is that?"

The jailer's face turned pale. "Lord Zenega is the King's advisor, but we believe he is a sorcerer and holds the King in his power," the jailer said in a low voice.

"How long has this Zenega been here?"

"Since the King was a young man, and *they* came. Zenega made the peace with *Them* in the name of the King."

"Who . . . are *They*?"

The jailer's cheek and right eye twitched uncontrollably. He reached for a chair, pulled it up to the cell, and sat on it. Frightened and trembling, the man spoke in a hoarse whisper, looking over his shoulder.

"Long ago, our land was peaceful and bountiful. The children played happily in the fields, and everyone had nary a want. One day, Lord Zenega arrived at the castle. In a short time, most people believed Lord Zenega must have cast a spell on the King.

"The air changed, the crops dried up, and joy left the people. Then, an evil thing came one day from nowhere. One night in late October, when the moon was full in the sky, *They* burned our homes, destroyed our crops, killed our animals, and took our children. The King was powerless.

The knights tried to stop *Them* but got eliminated.

"Then more knights, soldiers, and men from everywhere came on quests to stop *Them*. The evil devoured them as well. Lord Zenega promised the King that if he wouldst swear to make and keep a covenant of peace, he would see *They* would no longer harm the people of this land. Even after the older king had died and the prince became king and took the throne, nothing has ever happened again."

"Why do you say that? Is there no longer any threat from *Them*?"

"So long as Zenega has his way, there is peace. When Zenega becomes angered, they come . . . and many things get destroyed."

"Does Zenega get angry often?"

"Aye. But no one has seen *them* for a long time. Every autumn, *they* come looking for the young girls . . . but it is said the girls run off to Audra, a good witch, who protects them."

"Who is Audra?" Doug inquired.

"She was once a sorceress. She was born to sorcerers who were good and kind to the Kingdom until they died. When Audra was old enough, she became the queen sorcerer. Then Zenega came and cast a spell on her. The King sentenced her to burn at the stake for interfering with the autumn harvest of girls. She escaped into the woods, never to be heard from again."

"Why are young girls sought every year?"

"The young girls? Aye, they are for Lord Zenega. They keep him content, I suppose."

"What happened to the other girls he had from years past?"

"No one knows. All have disappeared. Some still believe those still alive are somewhere in the castle here. That is why the maidens run to the hills and the knights have to hunt them. The daughters of the people at court enjoy privileges.

"How long must the girls hide?"

"For a fortnight, until the last day of October has come. Then, Lord Zenega's madness is past."

"What happens if they don't find any young girls?"

"*They* will come upon us until we deliver at least one."

"What madness is Zenega possessed of?"

"No one knows. No one sees Zenega until after the madness passes."

"Where in the castle does Zenega live?"

"He has the entire northwest corner and the highest tower."

"Is the tower his place of sorcery?"

"Many believe it to be."

"Does he live alone?"

"Nay, he has his Red Guards around him, ruthless men who would as soon slit yer throat as look at ya."

"Are there a lot of them?"

"Aye, about twenty to thirty, maybe more. Zenega brought them with'im."

"Do they look for the women, too?"

"Nay ... heh, they wouldn't arrive virgins, now wouldst they?"

Doug thanked the jailer. Then, while he turned to face the men, he had a second thought.

He turned back and asked, "By the way, you never really told me who or what are *they*, that everyone is so terri . . ."

Doug never finished his question. The request to clarify "*they*" was too much for the rotund jailer. His eyes rolled back into his head, and he fainted. Then he fell off his chair and into a heap on the floor. The men heard the clanking of metal on metal coming from the passageway.

"Someone's coming," Bailey whispered.

"No shit, Sherlock," Vinnie responded, causing Bailey to give him a dirty look.

Nine men dressed in red uniforms armed with swords walked into the enclosure. They saw the jailer on the floor and the four prisoners still in their cell.

"Check the door," the one most likely to be the leader said.

"It's still locked," another one said.

"Open it," the leader said.

Another reached down, removed the keys on the jailer's belt, and unlocked the cell door

They rushed in, grabbed the crewmen, and dragged them into the open enclosure, pinning them against the walls. When the men struggled, the Red Guards pulled whips off the wall and flogged them until they stopped resisting. Again, the Red Guardsmen pinned them against the wall and held them there. Even Doug found their strength to be overpowering. Although the crewmen had cuts and bled, their faces continued to show defiance. Slapping a horse crop against his palm, the leader looked each man over before speaking.

"My lord and I don't know who you are, but before the King has every one of you burned at the stake, I want some answers," the leader said. "Who sent you here?" He asked Vinnie.

"Go suck an egg dipstick," Vinnie replied.

The two men holding Vinnie forced his arms behind him while the leader slapped him across the face with the riding crop. Then he kicked Vinnie in the groin, causing him to double over. When Vinnie fell to the floor, the two guards kicked him violently in the ribs many times, leaving Vinnie in a heap, coughing and sputtering.

Doug yelled at them to stop, but got punched in the stomach and the face by the leader. Then Boz and Bailey struggled with their guards and suffered more of the same whipping by the cat-o'-nine-tails. The captain of the guard arrived unexpectedly to make a last check on the prisoners, saw what the Red Guards were doing, and ordered them to stop.

"I'm here by order of Lord Zenega to interrogate these prisoners," the leader said arrogantly.

"You will do no such thing," the captain commanded. "I have sole authority here, and Lord Zenega knows that. Get out before I summon my men."

"We're not finished with these . . . these . . .vermin yet. We will have our way with them one way or another," the leader said, looking defiantly into the captain's eyes, which caused a slight shiver to go through him.

"Put them back into the cell," the captain ordered.

Deciding not to further inflame an already tense relationship with the castle guards, the leader nodded, and his men complied, leaving the enclosure. Glaring at the prisoners, the leader left last. The captain locked the cell door and left. The old jailer still lay on the floor, passed out.

"I'm gonna kill that son of . . ." Vinnie said, still in pain and coughing.

"Vinnie!" Bailey yelled as he ran to his side, followed by Boz and

Doug.

"Look! His mouth is bleeding," Boz said.

"Yeah, I bet his insides aren't doing any better," Bailey said.

"Vinnie, can you move?" Doug asked.

"I think it's time to grab the straps and eject outta here," Boz exclaimed.

The men had overheard the conversation between Doug and the jailer. He knew this sorcerer's madness enveloped them. Doug believed he and the crew could find themselves at a barbecue dinner for whomever they were. The beating they had received by a bunch of Gestapo-looking goons who would hammer them to death if they felt like it was a good sign.

"Yeah, I think so," Vinnie groaned.

"Okay, we need to get outta here before someone returns to replace the old man. Does anybody have something to pick this lock with?" Doug asked.

Bailey pulled his Swiss Army knife from his pants pocket and went to work. It didn't take long to open the ancient locking device. The door swung open freely, and the men exited.

"Hey, wait . . . what about the jailer?" Asked Boz.

"Drag him into the cell," ordered Doug. "Okay, men. Let's take it real slow and carefully. Remember, if we get caught, it's curtains."

"It's curtains, no matter what we do," Vinnie groaned, holding his midsection.

Chapter X

Within the frosty air of his damp, dark dungeon-like study made of stone, Lord Zenega sat behind his favorite desk, made of alabaster with opaque striations of silver and gray. Beside the sorcerer sat his new, weasel-like assistant, Melonjack. They'd eavesdropped intently on the King's interrogation of the prisoners. Melonjack wore a brown scapular with a hood.

When Zenega first arrived and took up residence in his corner of the castle, he discovered a tubing system that ran through the walls and no one had ever completed it. Small, carved stone bear heads capped the ends of the tubing system. But no one ever put them in the dungeons or the secret passages.

He created listening devices connected by these tubes and placed them in every significant room in the castle. He enjoyed the ability to eavesdrop and give the impression he knew information beforehand, adding to the myth he had clairvoyance. The device operated on an air tube principle.

After interviewing the prisoners, he knew the King would have gone to his room. He would want to discuss the newfound threats to the peace with his wife. Zenega had decided, for the Kingdom's good, that the prisoners' execution by burning at the stake was a foregone conclusion since they were not nobility.

The four men's friends might never learn of their fate. Besides, a similar fate awaited him if anyone else came looking for them. He'd summon his friends to convince them otherwise if these retributions didn't discourage outsiders from following their curiosity.

Zenega effectively used his room on the top floor of the northwest tower. It was a typical sorcerer's room with wooden shelves lined with books on black magic. Charts and beakers of potions filled every space along the walls.

Above: From the low ceiling hung a large globe of the earth and an assortment of astronomic symbols. A good-sized telescope rested on the northern windowsill and faced the moon. A large stone laboratory table sat in the room.

When the autumn season dominated the days before the great harvest, Zenega fell into his foulest moods. An affliction seized him he understood, but dared not divulge. He led a double life . . one human and one not.

The constant pain inside his head drove him mad, to where he wanted to jump off the top of the tower. No potion existed to cure this madness, which fell upon him at the full moon of each October.

The madness led him into uncontrollable rages, in which he yelled and screamed at anyone who laid sight of him. His eyes burned red-hot, his skin turned pale, and his mouth foamed like a mad dog's. The madness lasted only for brief spells, coming less frequently since he moved to Xanpathia.

Walking along a rampart, Zenega recalled when he'd first arrived. Back then, the realm had been celebrating the anniversary and the feast of the crowning of King Vigero. Zenega had presented himself at court and offered the new king spiritual guidance and worldly knowledge . . . if the King would provide him quarters inside the castle.

The King had thanked the wise man but politely declined, citing a breach in court etiquette and approving the court of lords; also, he said he already had a skilled spiritual guide named Audra attending to his needs. Zenega had felt extreme outrage at this rebuff. He vowed to himself to change the King's mind soon.

Zenega had had his eye and desires cast on Audra since he first saw her radiant beauty. She taunted his ego; he needed to possess her in every way, but she rebuffed him. He vowed revenge on them all.

At the full moon the following month, Zenega called upon his friends, who flew in with the north wind and arrived with the Red Guard. After the evil pillaged, plundered, and devastated the people and their crops, the King availed himself to anyone who could rid his kingdom of this menace. Audra proved powerless against this new menace.

When Zenega reappeared at court and again offered his services, the King took a much more humble and generous attitude, provided that Zenega would fulfill his promise. When peace came, Zenega stood before the King and politely expected to receive his reward of a set of rooms in the castle and a place at court.

The King instead gave Zenega an entire wing and knighted him. Zenega, seizing this opportunity, also introduced his household, Red Guards. He told the King he needed his Red Guards for security so he would not impose on the King's resources. A pious thought, but acceptable.

In time, Zenega cast spells over the countryside and the King. His attempts to persuade the people through witchcraft had become a much bigger feat, even for the great sorcerer. But the King, the head of state, was sufficient for Zenega's diabolical purposes.

Zenega, through his sorcery, rid the Kingdom of all spiritual joy practices, and Audra then ensconced himself as the primary influence behind the King. Anyone who opposed him mysteriously ended up dead from some unknown cause. Insiders believed the Red Guard untrustworthy, given their nefarious activities, but no one convinced the King to investigate.

Alas, the King languished and became captivated by Zenega's spell, falling under his total control. Zenega became the actual power behind the throne, even after Vigero died and the young Alexander became crowned. Zenega had a personal agenda. He needed to convince the new king. He desired a few young girls to quell the annual madness that befell him when they came to the age of consent.

At first, the King refused, saying it was an immoral and despicable request. He feared the Kingdom might rebel. But Zenega resorted to using his resources to get what he wanted, and the King eventually agreed.

They returned to enforce his dictates when the madness overtook the great sorcerer. To prove his point, one year, when the eligible maidens fled into the hills and woods and hid, Zenega recalled *them* to ravage the countryside until a girl came before him.

No matter what retributions Zenega imposed or threatened, the parents of these girls defied him. They continued encouraging their daughters to take to the hills and woods yearly. To take the chance that the onus wouldn't befall one of them to become the consort of the sorcerer.

Zenega instructed his vassals that a seized girl first went to the caves east of the valley. He'd quickly travel there to perform a ritual where he put the girl into an endobiotic state. After Zenega finished with her, he would house her in a room in the farthest corner of his living quarters for a purpose only he knew and intended to keep to himself.

The guard at the door properly announced the King and offered him a seat near the fireplace.

"So, Your Majesty, what brings you to my humble residence? Your newfound trespassers, perhaps?" Zenega inquired.

"You are truly a wizard, Lord Zenega. It is true. I seek your council as to their fate."

"Why so, Your Majesty? It appears they are here to breach the peace. I see no reason to allow them to live. Put them at the stake and be done with them."

"Are we sure they are, not who they say they are?" The King asked.

"And who are they? Soldiers, knights, some others who have come into your kingdom on a quest? No, my liege, no matter who they are and what reason they give. You must destroy them to preserve the peace. We must let all who enter this realm without permission know we intend to arrest them."

"So be it. As for the autumn festival, I have prepared a grand feast."

Zenega felt the onset of the madness slowly rise inside him and told the King in a controlled but harsh tone, "I don't care about the feast. What I require are the girls you promised me. Now leave me."

No stranger to Zenega's mad spells, the King took his leave without another word. After he returned to his side of the castle, the King sent for the palace guard commander.

General Gaiet arrived within five minutes of receiving the summons. He gave absolute loyalty to the King. As an example of his dedication and for his purposes, he quietly identified those who were Lord Zenega's spies within the palace guard and alerted his officers to their identities.

Many years ago, guidelines differentiated between the palace guard and the castle knights. The ornately dressed soldiers who served the King took responsibility for events mostly inside the eighteenth-century palace.

The earliest kings decreed medieval knights. Medieval soldiers took responsibility for the events that occurred mostly outside and around the castle and villages. The household cavalry took jurisdiction wherever they wanted. They faithfully carried out the duties of the King's constabulary.

The good general carried no influence over the knights of the realm. They answered only to the King and did his bidding outside the castle. The general, short and chubby with greasy black hair, wore a pencil-thin mustache.

General Gaiet had a reputation for his expertise with a blade. Onetime before Zenega's arrival . . . he had given the young king's father many hours of instruction on the finer points of the art of fencing. But that was ancient history, and no longer played a part in today's reality.

The general felt no fondness for the sorcerer, and the King knew this. Yet because of the general's undying loyalty, having him near gave the King a secure feeling.

"You called me, my liege?" The general asked as he walked to the King's desk, holding his helmet in his left arm and saluting with his right.

"Yes, I did, General. I have decided the four men brought to me are here to break the peace. Therefore, I have ruled those strange men are to be executed by burning at the stake at sundown tomorrow night. I want you to arrange it."

"Yes, Your Majesty. But where are they to be put to death . . . inside the castle or outside? And do you wish to invite the villagers?"

"Outside, at the usual place near the river, so the stench flows over the villagers and not us."

"As you wish, Your Majesty. I will see to the preparations."

"And put some guards on them. One jailer is not a comfort to me."

"Consider it done, Your Majesty. Will there be anything else?"

"René, why are you so formal tonight?"

"If I may speak freely, my liege? I know these people are no harm to us, yet Lord Zenega, and not you, has condemned them to death. I see no purpose in this."

"René, I am too tired to argue with you tonight. I have a queen and princess yet to argue with, and the thought of that removes my will to discuss this decision's merits right now. But that does not mean I wish to ignore your council; perhaps later, René."

"As you wish, Your Majesty." The general left and went to the quarters of the captain of the night detail, David Bedwell, who was carefully reading his reports before he forwarded them for review. When he saw who had walked into his office, the captain jumped to attention. The general told Captain Bedwell of the King's wishes for additional guards for the prisoners and left the quarters.

Captain Bedwell called the sergeant of the guard and told him he wanted two guards detailed for duty on the prisoners. The sergeant immediately went to the night guard's quarters and assigned two guards to the dungeon rooms. The guards dressed and departed for their assignment.

´Chapter XI

His Majesty paced the floor of his apartment. In a matter of speaking, he became engrossed in a crisis he wished he didn't have to deal with and would escape from if there were any means available to him. He went over what he knew in his mind.

After a morning ride, the queen caught the princess in the close embrace of a newly knighted young man. They had been in the stable without parental consent or escort.

The queen wants us to confront the princess and deny her the opportunity to play one parent against the other. It was the queen's insistence that the princess respond to the question about her virtue. The princess, who takes after her mother in terms of cunning, naturally evaded the question by asking another question and making an accusation against her mother of everything short of high treason.

Nearly sixteen, Princess Rebecca sat alone in her room, looking into a mirror, examining her fair white skin and her cheeks' natural pinkness.

She sported the blondest hair anyone had ever seen in a girl. Her not-so-cheerful round face, adorned with two big, steel-blue eyes, could freeze forever a man she wished to scorn.

Unfortunately, she knew men showed more interest in her ample endowments than her face. As the princess, she knew she was untouchable by anyone who valued their family jewels. Any advances made toward her would never meet with her parents' approval, but received a certain reproach.

As for her new young knight, she knew he hadn't learned simple court etiquette since knights of the court didn't require such training. Their place was in the large hall behind the castle where men stressed manhood and knighthood and where dainties weren't welcome and got laughed out.

Enamored by her new boyfriend, she quickly acquainted herself with the knight's living area, decorated in a purely medieval setting. The colony of knights intended to keep it their way. The knights' status stood no lower or higher than the nobles at court. It was merely a different lifestyle. For one group, the way of real men, the knights; and for the other, one of fineness, the castle dwellers.

She quickly grew weary of gentlemen suitors who partook in the social graces from afar but ventured no closer lest they get scrutinized by her mother and father. But knights were real, rough-and-tumble men with a dragon-slaying mentality. That's what attracted her to them. They refused to take part in social graces and refinement and had no restraint in wooing a woman, any woman.

Pacing back and forth in her room, she thought.

I am the princess, Rebecca Ann, named after my paternal grandmother and mother. I am a daughter of the House of Darpon, the dynasty that rules the castle and the realm. I have inherited my parents' lusts and passions, and I unashamedly let them overrule my better judgment, even at fifteen.

She knew anyone who might deflower her before marriage would earn his instant death, and she wasn't stupid enough to let something like that happen. Yet, she had no problem experimenting with her eighteen-year-old, newly knighted boyfriend.

Princess Rebecca felt a lot of anger toward her mother for banishing her to her room. She thought she was not insolent and felt it was within her right to refuse to answer her parents' questions. At this moment, Rebecca decided she'd endured enough of their disrespect and intended to run away. Where to? She didn't know or have any idea. But she knew she planned to leave and live her own life in her own way.

Unfortunately, she also knew she was naïve and ignorant of the outside world's ways. She rarely received permission to venture away from the castle. The first thought that came to her was,

How do I get out of the castle without being seen? Her second thought was, *how do I survive once I'm out? And where do I go?*

Those obstacles alone might cause enough despair to deter anyone, but they were not impossible for her. She plotted how to get out of the castle. Rebecca vaguely remembered that she had once overheard her mother talking to someone many years ago.

She couldn't remember who it had been. They'd reminisced about how when her mother was a teenager. Before she had married her father, the queen-to-be used to explore the secret passages that ran throughout the castle.

Rebecca remembered overhearing her mother telling her friend how she used to peek in on the young prince through a spy hole she'd found in a wall bordering his room. Rebecca, too young to understand such things, gave no further thought to the conversation . . . until this very moment.

If there were secret passages, was there an entrance to them from her room? She looked around. She pressed spots on the walls, and when that yielded no results, she pulled on things or pushed on things.

Finally, she felt defeated as she walked past the hearth in her room. She noticed stone-carved lion's faces with large shiny brass rings in their noses on each corner under the mantle.

I never remember seeing these brass rings before. Rebecca grabbed the left one. It flopped up and down within the ring holder. She tried twisting it, but it wouldn't move. Then she tried to pull on it, and it moved away from the stone a fraction of an inch . . . no more, but it was a sufficient amount to expose part of a heavy chain link.

Now, she instantly felt her interest piqued. She took the ring with both hands and pulled on it with all her might. The ring extended the length of about two chain links, but no more. She felt convinced there was something more to this ring.

Rebecca placed her feet on either side below the lion's face on the wall, grasped the ring, and pulled with every ounce of strength. She took a giant step up the wall, virtually placing the entire length of her body parallel to the floor.

The old chain inched ever so slightly, creaking and groaning. When it did, Rebecca's head drooped toward the floor. After a moment, her body stretched out horizontally, making the back of her head touch the floor. The chain extended about two feet farther. The fire pit within the hearth rotated ninety degrees, making many grinding noises.

She let go of the chain and excitedly got up from the floor. She ran to the table in her bedroom and grabbed a lantern-like oil lamp off the wrought iron holder. Her heart racing, she entered the dark, dank passage full of cobwebs behind the fire pit.

She stopped and wondered for a minute.

Where does this passage go? If it leads to an escape, I'm not dressed for this.

Rebecca went back to her bedroom and undressed. She took out her riding britches, boots, and a heavy sweater. Rebecca thought, you can't run around in a dress, and it's getting cold outside. After properly attiring herself and putting her golden blond hair in a ponytail, she went back into the passageway.

She observed another ring and chain hanging from the inside of the upper wall. Another ring and chain hung from the bottom of the wall. She surmised correctly that the chain with the slack was open and that the ring without the slack on the bottom of the wall closed the secret entrance.

Rebecca pulled on the ring, and the hearth closed. She marked her room with a stone she found on the floor. She then went along the passageway in the direction she guessed led to the front of the castle, to the right of the hearth's position. The passageway went straight and passed a flight of stairs every forty paces. She walked along the passage and noticed intervals within the walls. At the seams, she discovered small, built-in spy holes. Peering into one, she looked down a dark hallway. Rebecca saw a torch on a wall, illuminating what seemed to be a passageway beyond. She explored the walls more and found outlines of secret doors like the one in her room. She guessed there were also ways from other rooms to enter and exit the passageways without detection.

Rebecca put that in the back of her mind for now. She'd figure out what to do about this discovery at some other point. All she desired now was to escape from this dreadful life and this awful castle.

She eventually came to a dead-end and a door. To the right, a set of steps led down below. Rebecca estimated it exited under the first floor since the number of steps she descended amounted to more than those going to her room.

But she wasn't sure. She knew it felt colder and damper here than at the higher levels of the passageway. The adrenaline pumped through her body like a wild mustang. The exhilaration of doing something unnatural excited her beyond comprehension. A small door at the bottom of the steps, built about two feet off the floor, had room enough for one person to squeeze through.

It had two bolt mechanisms, one on the top and one on the bottom, with a small wooden beam for additional security across the door's width. Rebecca placed the lantern on the steps and unbolted the door slowly while removing the wooden beam. She pulled on the handle, and the door slowly agonized with high-pitched creaking sounds as it opened.

With significant resistance, it eventually gave way to the determined young woman. Rebecca immediately felt a frigid blast of air wrap around her face and cause a sting. She smelled the odor of the moldy, dank sewer coming through the opening. At first, she thought she was looking into the darkness of night.

When she opened the door even wider, she grabbed her lantern and saw a small landing and a staircase to its left. It was narrow and allowed little room to move around. She closed the door and descended the stairs with her lantern until she reached another landing, with an archway to the right.

She walked a few feet on the landing, and an opening appeared to her left, followed by another small flight of stairs. Looking down a few steps, she immediately recognized the walls of the sewer. Freedom's call beckoned her.

Rebecca entered the quick-flowing water, which came up to her calves. She turned right and walked through the water to the end of the tunnel, where she saw the glimmer of the last remnants of sunset. She discovered an iron gate attached to the brick wall to protect the castle from intruders.

Rebecca felt trapped, like a prisoner in a dungeon. Panic seeped into her mind, but she forced herself to put it aside and figure a way out. She put her lantern down on a flat protrusion extending from the stone wall, then looked and felt around for something to use to break the lock on the gate. After a few moments, she found a large rock.

She quickly picked up the heavy stone and took it over to the edge of the gate. With great determination, she raised the rock over her head with both hands and brought it crashing down on the lock. She missed her intended target.

Again, with more incredible determination, she raised the rock over her head, held it long enough to get a good aim, and brought it down.

This time, it crashed into the lock, breaking off its heavy, rusted iron hasp. The gate swung open, and with caution, she climbed into the drainage ditch, which emptied into the stream that paralleled the castle.

Princess Rebecca noticed the sun had nearly set to her right, letting her know she was facing south and headed toward the crop fields on the other side of the stream.

She turned off her lantern so she would draw no attention to herself and made her escape official. Rebecca headed for the forest through the crop fields and thought about where to go. She left the lantern on a short wall at the mouth of the sewer.

´Chapter XII

D oug led the way through the dungeon room door and up the stairs to the dining room. Since there was no window in the second door, he cracked it open and peeked inside. He heard voices. About ten armed men sat at the tables, eating; their uniforms identified them as the palace guards.

"Well, we're not going this way," he said as he gently closed the door.

"What's up?" Vinnie asked.

"The palace guards are dining. Let's go back and find another way," Doug said.

When they returned to the dungeon room, he told the men to look for any other way out. Under the jailer's table, Boz found a small grating about the size of a manhole cover. The men pulled the table away and pulled on the grating with their fingers; it seemed immovable. Doug spotted an iron pike mounted on the wall. He took it down and used it on the grate like a crowbar.

After a lot of huffing and puffing, the grate gave way, and the men prepared to explore the possibility of this alternative route. Bailey monitored the dungeon room door and heard the upper dining-room door squeaking open.

"We got company coming," Bailey urgently warned in a loud whisper.

"Grab the torches, and let 'em have it when they come in," Doug ordered.

Vinnie and Boz grabbed a torch; the room had one mounted on each wall. Bailey returned to the others and stood near Doug. They had no way of knowing who was coming or how many. The creaky old wooden door opened, and two Napoleonic-era-dressed guards entered the room. Boz and Vinnie greeted them with a blow to the head.

Doug grabbed one, rendering him unconscious with one good punch to the jaw. Bailey helped Vinnie take the second one out. The men stripped the guards of their weapons and put them in the same cell as the jailer.

"Everyone grab a torch, and let's get down the sewer," Doug ordered.

"Vinnie, replace that pike so they can't figure out how we escaped." Bailey, the shortest of the group, went down the ladder first. Luckily, there were built-in metal rungs to climb down. When Bailey reached the bottom, he found a red brick wall using his flashlight. It was a semi-cylindrical-shaped sewer tunnel he estimated to be about seven feet high and seven feet wide. He noticed about a foot of water flowing through the sewer.

Bailey waited for the rest of the crew to descend before scouting ahead. Doug and Vinnie crawled into the hole and pulled the table over them.

Doug pulled the grate into its open position. He prayed that when the other guards discovered the escape, their route through the bowels of the castle would remain a secret.

Doug led the men carefully through the sewer. They recognized the smell of dank rainwater permeating the sewer and were glad it wasn't raw sewage.

"I'm not a civil engineer and, therefore, am not familiar with these things. As a historian, I know there were no sewers as elaborate as this in castles built in the medieval period," Doug commented.

"I think we've traveled about twenty to thirty yards by now," Boz estimated.

They reached an intersection and were unsure which way to go. Boz took out his compass and pointed to the right, showing the way out. Vinnie went on ahead to scout the passage.

In a few moments, he came rushing back and reported, "I found the opening. It reaches a small stream about twenty yards from the castle wall. The creek runs parallel to the south wall. There are fields on the other side, and I think we should kill the torches so they can't see us."

"I agree. Let's get'em out, men, but leave'em hidden near the mouth of the sewer," Doug ordered.

The crewmen proceeded to the end of the sewer in total darkness until Vinnie helped them one at a time into the moonlit evening. They noticed the iron gate protecting the sewer exit had broken and swung free.

"Watch your step. The sewer empties into this stream, so we're gonna get our feet wetter than they are now," Vinnie whispered.

When each crewman stepped into the small stream, Doug took the torches and the confiscated weapons and hid them under the brush. The air had gotten cold, and Doug suggested the crewmen button up their BDU shirts. Doug crossed the stream and found a small line of trees on the embankment that paralleled the stream.

He saw the castle lit up behind them, like some amusement park; it seemed very unusual, even if it was by torchlight. Doug gathered his men around him.

"According to my little compass, we must go west and south to get back into the forest and make our way to the tank. There's an irrigation canal that flows north-south and follows the road. The terrain's flat grassland and farm fields go from here to the edge of the forest, which I estimate is about three or more miles. I figure it will take us two to three hours to make it because of obstacles, so let's move. And don't get lost! Stay together."

Doug encouraged the men to get moving across the fields. The moon sat high in the clear sky. All that illumination made it a lousy route for escape and evasion. Open fields were the only terrain there was to cross. Doug guided the men along the borders of the fields and hedgerows. He wanted to keep the view of their silhouettes to a minimum. He kept looking over his shoulders, waiting for horsemen to ride down on them.

The sergeant of the guard looked at his hourglass and saw it was time to relieve the dungeon guards. He called for two men to take over until the next relief arrived. The two guards proceeded to the dungeon chamber and opened the door to find no one, and the room was dark.

"That's queer," one guard said.

"Where have they gone off to?" The other said as both stood in the dark.

The first guard went up the stairs and brought back a lit torch. They checked the cells until they found the open cell with the two unconscious guards and the jailer. They both ran to the dining room and through the door to find the sergeant of the guard.

"Sir, the prisoners have escaped, and the old jailer and two palace guards appear knocked out in the vacant cell."

Bloody hell, the sergeant thought. I need to alert Captain Linden. No, later. It's my head. I'll order the entire guard detail turned out to look for the prisoners within the castle.

As the search began, he went to the captain, informed him of what had happened, and said he had ordered a complete search of the castle.

The captain expressed his displeasure with the report, but he commended the sergeant for his initiative. The captain called on Lieutenant Terrine of the household cavalry and issued orders to prepare for a search of the castle grounds. He also sent a runner to fetch the keeper of the hounds if he needed to use them.

General René Gaiet indulged himself in a delusion of grandeur. He was reading a book on famous cavalry charges, figuring out ways he would have done it better, when the loud, intruding knock came at his door. The general, already in a distressed mood, opened the door to his apartment. He saw his captain of the guard with a furious look on his face.

"They've escaped, General."

"Whaaat?" the general asked, his mouth dropping open slowly as the word came out in a long drawl.

"How can this be, Captain?"

"I am told that when my sergeant of the guard sent the relief down to the dungeon, they found the room dark and two palace guards and the jailer in a cell, unconscious."

"What steps did you take to find the prisoners?"

"In the event they are still within the castle, I have turned out the guard and the horse cavalry to begin a search. I have also alerted the master of the hounds to be ready to put the dogs on them if we need to."

"Good. For now, let's keep this to ourselves. I see no need to alert the King at this hour."

"I agree, my general. I will keep you informed of our progress."

The captain saluted the general and left. General Gaiet considered the possibility that the prisoners had made it outside the castle walls. He needed to prepare for that likelihood.

A Red Guard detail observed the King's men scurrying around in sheer panic while making their evening rounds. The leader accosted a nearby knave and asked what the commotion was about. He told them of the escape, and they immediately went to tell Zenega.

Chapter XIII

Doug figured they'd traveled about a mile from the castle and hoped their escape had remained undiscovered. He expected men on horseback to come looking for them at any minute. Doug prodded his men to hurry, his anxiety showing in his voice. Flashbacks of his escape from the North Vietnamese fueled his anxiety.

"Hey, sarge, you're wearing us out! Can't we ease up a bit?" Boz pleaded.

"Not until we're safely in the forest," Doug responded. "You boys don't know what it feels like to be hunted. It's an experience you'll never forget, believe me."

"That happen to you in Nam, sarge?" Bailey inquired.

"Never mind, just keep moving," Doug blurted.

Doug heard the faint sounds of barking dogs in the distance behind them and saw the twinkles of torch lights, probably carried by men on horseback.

"I guess they've discovered we're gone. The dogs must have picked up our scent," Doug remarked. "I told you we needed to hurry. I hope we can get into the woods before they catch up to us."

Right then, Vinnie tripped over a large pile of hay and fell on top of someone. "Hey, what the hell . . . my god, it's a girl!" Vinnie gasped.

"Who are you!" The girl demanded.

"My name is Vinnie . . . and who are you, and what are you doing here?" Vinnie asked as he got to his feet while pulling the girl by her arm out of the haystack.

"We've got no time for this, kids . . . the hounds will be upon us in no time, and we need to make tracks," Doug said as Boz and Bailey caught up.

"What's your name, honey, and what are you doing out here?"

"Uh . . my name is Rebecca, and I'm running away from home," she said petulantly.

"Great, now we have a runaway teenybopper bubble gummer to deal with. Sarge, she'll get us caught if we linger," Boz said.

"Well, we can't leave her; she'll give away our position if they find her, so she goes with us. Get your asses in gear, and move!" Doug ordered.

Vinnie took the girl by the hand and helped her get moving.

"Who is that man ordering everybody?" She asked Vinnie.

"That's our sergeant; he's our boss, and he knows what he's doing. And why on earth is a cutie like you running away from home? You're not a farm girl dressed like that," Vinnie observed.

"I've had enough of my parents telling me what to do, who I can and can't see, and I'm just fed up. So, I've left home," she puffed while she hurried along with Vinnie.

"How old are you?" Vinnie asked.

"Fifteen," she said.

"Fifteen! Christ, you're still jailbait!" Vinnie blurted.

"What's jailbait?" She inquired innocently.

"Never mind, I forgot where I was."

"And what's a . . a . . .teenybopper . . . and a bubble gummer?"

"That's what we call fifteen-year-olds where we come from," Vinnie answered.

"Where exactly do you come from? I've never seen men like you before dressed like . . . like trees."

"It's called a BDU; I mean, a battle dress uniform," Vinnie explained.

"But you're not knights. So, does that mean you're soldiers of some kind?"

"Yes, we are soldiers of some kind who got lost and ended up in your country, wherever the hell this place is," Vinnie said, frustrated by the inquisitive teenager.

Doug led the men and Rebecca deeper into the fields from the roadway. He found cornfields to mask them as they continued to head south. They saw the cavalrymen racing along the road in both directions, attempting to find any sign of the escapees.

The searchers spread the hound dogs across the crop fields, where they were barking and whining as they tugged on their leashes. Doug figured that if they traveled through the wet cornfields, their human scents might dilute, causing the dogs to lose track of them. Then, by chance, they came upon an irrigation ditch, and Doug ordered everyone to get into it and continue walking east.

Vinnie still held Rebecca under tow and made himself her temporary guardian. *She's adorable*, he thought, with all that blond hair in a ponytail and those tight riding breeches accentuating her small derriere and those bodacious . . . Vinnie returned his concentration immediately to escaping and evading their pursuers and away from his carnal thoughts toward a fifteen-year-old.

Doug ordered everyone to get out about three hundred meters along the ditch, and the crew headed south again. He knew they were still nearly two miles from the nearest tree line.

While walking briskly, Vinnie asked Rebecca, "And what, pray tell, were you doing in that pile of hay?"

"I was tired and sat down for a minute," she replied, "until you fell on me and scared me. For a moment, I thought I got caught."

"Where were you planning on going?"

"I don't know . . . anywhere, just away from here," she said with a pout.

"It doesn't look like you thought this out very well. Does it? You have no food or protection against cold or bad weather and no idea where you're going."

"Neither do you," Rebecca taunted.

"We don't live here, Becky! You do, and you should at least have some idea of where you are and where you want to go," Vinnie hissed in her ear.

"Why did you call me Becky?"

"Where we come from, that's short for Rebecca. Haven't you ever heard of that nickname before?"

"No, I haven't; I haven't heard about many things, nor have I been let out of the castle very much, either."

"Geez, you live in the castle?"

"Yes, I do, and I can only go around freely inside; I have to use a chaperone or escort when I'm outside. That's how I got caught by my mother. I was in the stables where the knights live, visiting this boy I know. He was just knighted by my father a few weeks ago, and . . ."

"Whoa, girl, did you say your father knighted a boy?"

"Yes."

"Jesus Christ!" Vinnie yelled in a loud whisper.

"Your old man is the freaking king?" Then, with some hesitation, he continued. "Then that means you're a princess?"

"Um . . . THE princess," she said demurely. "I'm an only child."

The moonlight danced in Rebecca's happy, blue eyes, shining brightly and accenting a huge, childish smile.

"I think you're cute, Vinnie," she said, seductively giggling and scrunching her nose while squeezing his hand. Rebecca stood nearly eye to eye with Vinnie.

"Look, Rebecca, get any romantic notion you might foster about me out of your devious little mind right now," he whispered. He stopped taking her by the shoulders, put his nose to hers, and looked seriously into her eyes. She smiled ever wider, and Vinnie pulled his face back, knowing he was in deep trouble.

When Vinnie walked off, she grabbed his hand, ostensibly to keep up, but truthfully, she wanted to hold his hand. Rebecca had found a new love, and her face beamed brighter than the moon. She thought she would pursue this new found boy. The adventurousness had returned.

Chapter XIV

lex! She's disappeared!" The queen screamed in panic. "Impossible!" The King cried. "No, it's true. I just checked on Rebecca, and she wasn't there."

"She is probably being defiant, like you used to be, and is out with that young knight again; I'll have someone go look for her."

The King summoned Captain Linden of the evening guard detail. He ordered him to send a search party to locate the princess, saying she had most likely roamed into the knight's quarters. The captain saluted the King and went off to follow his orders.

Captain Linden assigned Sergeant Herbert (E-bare), saying, "Take four men and scour the area where the knights live and carouse. Find the princess and return her to me. If you receive any resistance, you will use whatever force you deem necessary to find her."

The King watched as the castle deteriorated into turmoil from his balcony. He saw every soldier, guard, and cavalryman take part in turning the place upside down, looking for the escaped prisoners. Then pandemonium broke loose when the additional orders came to look for the castle's royal adolescent.

When the King learned the initial searches had failed to produce the desired offenders, Captain Linden, as leader of the search parties, ordered everyone to go outside into the fields and head south. He'd ordered the hounds outside with the rest of the searchers to find a scent.

The knaves' initial reports showed so far they'd failed to pick up so much as a whiff. Captain Linden felt the strangers had likely intended to retrace their steps to where they began.

An hour later, Sergeant Herbert reported to Captain Linden, announcing, "Sir, I conducted a detailed search where everyone cooperated and still didn't find the princess." The captain then informed the King and queen.

"Well, she has to be somewhere," the queen moaned.

"I bet she has a hiding place. She has always kept secret that Rebecca goes to when she's mad at us. She'll come out when she gets hungry. You'll see," the King consoled.

"I hope you're right, Alex, because if anything happens to her, especially this time of the year, it will devastate me," warned Queen Ann. "Why don't you get off your royal throne and help look for her?"

"Now look, Ann . . ."

"Don't give me that 'now look, Ann' business! Can't you see how worried I am? Get dressed and go out and look for your daughter before something gets her," she fumed.

The King rose off his chair reluctantly and went into the bedroom to change clothes. He dressed in his riding apparel and left the apartment. The queen kept pacing the floor. A thought struck her, and she raced into Rebecca's room, opened the door, and went over to the hearth.

She grabbed the left ring on the lion's nose and pulled. The hearth swung open without resistance, and she took a candle and went inside the passageway. She bent down and saw fresh footprints far behind, confirming her suspicions. She returned to the room and pulled on the right ring to close the hearth.

The queen knew precisely where the passage went and where it ended. She returned to her room and pulled on the rope that summoned her senior servant. She jotted a note to Captain Linden. When the servant entered her chambers, she handed him the note.

"I want you to deliver this note to Captain Linden personally and then report to me to confirm the delivery."

The queen figured the princess most likely headed south across the farm fields to the forests to hide.

Doug and the group finally made it to the forest's edge through sheer determination. Even though the moon provided sufficient ambient light outside, the inside of the forest was pitch-black. The thickness of the trees allowed no moonlight to get through. Doug heard the hounds and guards getting closer.

"Rebecca, do you know of a path near here?" Doug asked.

"No, I've never been around here," she replied.

"Men, we must go to the left and away from the road along this tree line. Everybody, start moving to your left and cry out if you find a path leading into the forest," Doug ordered.

Fifteen minutes later, Bailey stopped and turned around, and in a loud whisper, he exclaimed, "Sarge, I found a path!"

Doug followed Bailey to the entrance into the forest, but he couldn't see over ten feet into the woods.

"Now what? We're stuck . . .unless we go on like the three blind mice or use our flashlights," Vinnie uttered, still attached to Rebecca's hand. Doug saw an object moving toward them without warning, glowing in the forest's darkness.

Doug yelled for everyone to take cover, drop to the ground, and find a hiding place. Vinnie pulled Rebecca on top of him and rolled her behind him to protect her. Bailey hid a few feet behind him.

"Bailey," Vinnie whispered.

"What?"

"Look, it's a glowing munchkin," Vinnie observed, amused.

The elflike figure walked to where everyone hid and stood there for a moment. The figure wore tight green leggings, a darker green pullover, and a long-sleeved shirt with a tunic over it decorated with sequins and other strange ornaments.

His slippers had turned-up, pointed toes. On his head sat a Robin Hood-styled hat. He stopped and waved his hand across the darkness, momentarily, everyone on both sides of the lit-up path.

"Come out, come out! I see you!" He sang.

Doug stood and walked toward him. The elf stood about three feet tall and was chubby. Doug noticed he wore a trim beard.

"What are you, a leprechaun?" Doug asked, looking at him.

The elf giggled. "What's a leprechaun?"

The rest of the crew and Rebecca got up off the ground and stood around Doug and the elf.

"Never mind. Who are you, and can you lead us to someplace in the forest where we can hide?" Doug asked.

"Sarge, how do you know he's not one of them?" Vinnie asked, pointing in the direction of the guards and the hounds.

"Vinnie, when have you ever known a munchkin to be a bad guy?" Bailey asked.

"What's a munchkin?" Rebecca whispered in Vinnie's ear.
Vinnie shot Rebecca an amused look. "Someone who looks like that," he whispered, tilting his head toward the elf.

"Your benefactor sent me to guide you through this enchanted forest," the elf said.

"Enchanted?" Boz queried.

"Never mind that! Look, whoever you are, the King's men are getting closer, and we have to get out of here," Doug pleaded.

"Come, follow me," the elf said as he walked along the path, lighting it naturally with the glow of his body.

"Won't the King's men see your glow when they get to the forest?" Boz asked the elf.

The elf didn't answer. Boz didn't know if the elf ignored him or didn't hear him, but he let it drop. As Doug and the group continued along the path, the sounds of their pursuers diminished. The glow from the elf revealed thick trees and undergrowth on both sides of the path, making it impassable at night and difficult during the day.

To Doug, it seemed like they walked most of the night. Slowly, hunger pangs affected his thoughts and, most likely, everyone else's. Fatigue and the need for sleep took their toll, too.

Finally, Doug asked, "Can we find a clearing and get some sleep or rest before going further?"

"Yes, let's walk a little further, then rest and sleep," the elf said.

After about another hundred yards, Doug and the group entered a large clearing with a small creek about ten yards to their right. Doug told the group to refresh themselves in the creek, find some soft undergrowth, and make themselves comfortable. In a few moments, the elf noticed everyone was fast asleep.

Rebecca snuggled with Vinnie and fell asleep with her head on his shoulder. The elf climbed a tree near him and settled into the crook of a branch. He pulled out a small amulet and spoke into it. "All's well," he said.

Chapter XV

Completely beside themselves, the King and queen paced around their apartment. They agonized over their missing daughter. The prisoners had now long escaped from the dungeon and might even have her with them.

The sorcerer had reverted to his usual foul mood, signaling the start of his annual spell of madness. The King and queen expected Zenega to call for his evil surrogates to begin a search for the elusive young girls, which added to their concern.

Captain Linden, the palace guards, the household cavalry, the bloodhounds, and all their knaves spent the night searching without one hint or clue of the whereabouts of the sought-after people. Linden dismissed them and instructed everyone to return at dawn and get some well-needed sleep. He told them he expected the search to continue later in the afternoon.

The King sought the sorcerer Zenega's wisdom. He appealed to him to use his talents to discover where his daughter and the prisoners were. Zenega told the King he couldn't bother with that and sent him away. Zenega had tried to use his sorcery to locate their whereabouts. Still, something blocked his attempts, and he could discover nothing.

He'd turned into an enraged animal when his crystals, bones, animal sacrifices, profound meditations, and spies failed to deliver one shred of information. As a last resort, he'd send his evil surrogates, his namatars, to search for the strangers . . . but at this very moment, it wasn't a top priority. He needed to satisfy his madness and lust first, and everything and everyone could wait until he felt gratified.

After the noon meal, Captain Bedwell, the captain of the guard of the day, assembled the search party. He issued orders to the knaves to return with their bloodhounds. Go into the forest and find a scent to pinpoint where the prisoners had entered.

Bedwell ordered the household cavalry to search the roads and villages throughout the realm. He ordered the knights to go with the knaves to provide protection and send word of their discoveries. He expected to continue the searches until sunset.

A cock crowed. Doug's eyes opened to see the sunlight probing through the wide overhangs of tree branches and leaves; déjà vu. Daybreak brought new anxieties for him, but it was time to wake up and move through the woods. Doug rose from his moss-and-leaf bed. He saw the elf perched on a thick tree branch, about ten feet off the ground.

He ignored him for the moment. Doug woke Boz and Bailey. As they got to their feet, he noticed Rebecca and Vinnie entwined like ivy and sound asleep.

"If only I had a camera. Angela would have an absolute fit, and Vinnie would become dead meat instantly," Bailey said with a big grin.

"Oh, stop, Bailey! I think they're cute together, even if she is jailbait," Boz said.

"She may very well be jailbait where we come from, but we're not back there, are we?" Doug said this as a statement and not a question, along with a wink and a grin.

The elf swung off the branch on which he'd perched and said, excitedly, "The hounds are heading toward the forest, which means the search for you and your friends continues. We must leave at once." Doug reached down and shook the two lovebirds.

"All right, you two, time to get up; we need to move."

Rebecca rolled over and looked around, confused. She needed to focus on her whereabouts. Vinnie jumped up like he'd gotten caught doing something with Rebecca he shouldn't have been doing.

"Okay, you two, we need to move," Doug ordered again. "The hounds have entered the forest!"

"Hey, how about some food? I'm starving," Vinnie declared.

"We don't have time to find you an IHOP right now. Maybe later," Doug said gruffly.

Vinnie reached for Rebecca, pulled her off the ground, and got her to walk. He brushed himself and Rebecca off and followed the elf along the path. The daylight allowed them to see the majestic beauty of this forest.

They saw trees with trunks so thick that four tall people couldn't get their arms around one. They saw vines with white flowers, bushes with yellow and red flowers, ferns, underbrush, and other vegetation.

"Where exactly are you taking us, my little friend?" Doug asked.

"To your benefactor," he replied.

"What benefactor?" Boz asked, concerned.

"The good witch, Audra . . . the good witch of the forest and all the land," the elf replied.

"Witch?" Vinnie said, stopping dead in his tracks.

The elf stopped and turned around. "Yes, the witch. She sent me to fetch you and your friends before the King's men found you."

"I feel a Hansel and Gretel moment coming," Vinnie lamented.

"C'mon, keep moving! We're toast if those bloodhounds find our trail," Doug warned.

After about an hour, Doug noticed the terrain slowly rising and the path getting steeper. After another hour, he recognized they had reached a plateau. Doug saw that the denseness of the forest was thinning out. He could see deeper into the woods, nearly one hundred yards.

Since they had no food or water, the elf stopped occasionally and pointed out pools of water and fruit growing wild to sustain themselves.

The elf eventually brought them to an open area surrounded by dense trees where they could see caves and a creek not too far. A large fire pit sat in the center of the clearing. There was still a small fire burning inside of it.

"We're here," the elf announced, showing that they had arrived at their destination.

"Sarge, I don't know where in the hell we are. My compass shows we're heading southwesterly," Vinnie announced.

"We need to figure out how to get back to Vicky," Doug said.

"Is that your iron war beast?" A voice said, echoing from inside the cave.

"Who said that?" Bailey asked, surprised.

A small, gnarly fingered old hag of a woman slowly came out from inside the cave, aided by a walking stick.

"You," she said, pointing her bony finger at Doug, "are the leader."

"Christ, she reminds me of Yoda," Vinnie whispered to Boz and Bailey.

"Yes, I am responsible for these men and this girl," replied Doug with caution in his voice.

"My name is Audra. I was once the sorceress of the realm . . . until Zenega arrived, and cast me out," she responded.

"Why were you cast out?" Rebecca asked innocently.

"Because I chose to save young girls like you, my child, instead of seeing them abducted every October fortnight to satisfy the bloodlust of Zenega's madness," Audra said.

"Why? I don't understand. Girls at the castle don't get abducted in October. The castle people get uneasy this time of the year, but I don't know anyone getting abducted," she said naively.

"And you must be Princess Rebecca, aren't you, my child?" Audra asked.

"I . . .ah . . .am, yes, Princess Rebecca," she said humbly. "How did you know?"

Audra's face revealed the warmth she felt inside her breast for the young girl. Then her eyes widened because she felt a premonition coming on, and their yellow jaundice became more visible.

"I know who you are because I saw you in my crystals. My child, you are in great danger," Audra told her, "along with the rest of your friends."

The witch turned, extended her right arm, palm up, and waved over the horizon, at which time about fifty young girls came out of the caves and woods dressed in peasant clothing.

Vinnie, Boz, and Bailey's mouths went agape. "Holy cow, we've died and gone to paradise!" Boz said in a shocked tone.

"Yeah, the seventy-two virgins are right before us," Bailey added.

"Or we're pawns in a cruel joke," Vinnie said dryly.

"Madam Audra, please explain where we are and why. You seem to know about our iron war beast, and we know nothing. What are all these young girls doing here?" Doug pleaded.

Audra invited everyone to sit down and have a rest. She then recounted her life story, explaining what had transpired since Zenega arrived. Audra told them what she'd done for these girls and their mothers before them for many years and what it eventually cost her. She explained Zenega had spared the royal family and the families of the realm's lords from his wrath. She looked over at Rebecca for a moment.

"Where do these abducted girls go, and what happens to them?" Boz asked, concerned.

"No one knows. I believe the girls get taken somewhere so Zenega can have his way with them. Then, they become gifts to the Red Guards. After a time, they go to the evil to devour. At least, that is what everyone now believes."

"Why are you crying, my child?" Audra asked.

"I'm so embarrassed about what my parents have caused, and I'm frightened for everyone's safety," she sobbed.

"Do not be ashamed, child. It was not your doing, and there is nothing you can do to change it," the good witch said.

"Look, Audra, what exactly do you think we can do for you? Why did you use your spells to bring us here?" Doug asked.

"I thought you and your men would be our champions," she offered.

"My dear, good woman . . . this is not a jousting match, where a knight champions a damsel to correct a wrong that, she feels a need for retribution," Doug replied.

"Nay, my good man, you are correct. It is a WAR! A war to the death. To save a kingdom from an evil that has plagued us for many years. And it will continue to plague us for eternity if someone or something does not stop it once and for all. Be not gallant, sir; there is no chivalry offered here. This scourge is war . . . cold, cruel, bloody, unadulterated WAR!" she said emphatically, leaning into his face, her foul breath contorting his expression.

"I have seen in my crystals and visions what your iron beast can do and what it has done. It is a savage beast and shows no mercy. Neither will this evil," she said.

"Is it your purpose to have us engage this evil of yours in battle?" Doug said, more than a statement than a question.

"If you do not, it will find and consume you when it senses and locates your presence," she said, "as a threat to its existence and to protect Zenega."

"How is it going to find us hiding out here?" Bailey asked sarcastically.

Another elf, unknown and not seen before, entered the clearing and slid down a long vine, announcing loudly, "The hounds have located the scent and are following it in this direction. I estimate they will arrive within a few hours."

Audra immediately tried to calm the girls, who nearly panicked after hearing the elf say. She told them to gather their belongings and to follow her to another hiding place. Then Audra turned to Doug.

"You must return to your iron beast and bring her to life again. She will lead you into a battle for righteousness and not forsake you, and you will be victorious," Audra assured them. "The lives of these girls, the princess, and I are in your hands."

"That's just great, lady. But how do we get to Vicky?" Vinnie said impatiently.

Audra ignored Vinnie's immature rant and turned her attention to Doug, saying, "I will send my most trusted elf to guide you to your war beast . . . your Vicky, was it?" She glanced back at Vinnie inquisitively. She drew a map in the dirt with her walking stick.

"You are northeast of your iron beast by nearly four leagues. The terrain is rough and difficult to pass through, so it will be hard to get back to the hut those knights found you in, but the elf will help you get there."

"Are you and the girls going to evade the King's men?" Doug asked.

"I will do what I can to protect the girls until you and the boys return," Audra said skeptically.

"What about the princess?" Vinnie asked. "I think she should come with us."

"No, my place is with everyone else," Rebecca said. "I am no different or any more special than they are. They have suffered and sacrificed while the other girls who live in the castle and I were safe and spared. Well, not anymore. Whatever happens to those girls happens to us equally, and if it costs my life, then so be it!"

Rebecca gave Vinnie a long, deep kiss, whispered, "I love you," and ran off.

"Okay, that answers the question of which direction we go to find Vicky," interjected Bailey. "Let's blow this pop stand and find her."

The other girls came over to the men. One by one, they gave the boys kisses, wished them good hunting, and ran off. Doug kissed Audra's hand and thanked her, and for a moment, her hand returned to normal before reverting to its ugly state. They looked into each other's eyes for a moment.

Doug saw a profound sadness, longing, and tiredness on her face. He understood, but didn't know what to do, much less say. Doug hated to leave the tired old woman, now reduced to a hag. But there wasn't anything he had the power to do except defeat this evil.

Audra saw a man with gallantry and chivalry, traits she'd never found in the men of the castle. It was why she had never gotten romantically attracted to anyone . . . until now, when it was too late for her.

She weakly squeezed his hand, said goodbye, and then turned to join her flock and flee before the King's men arrived. Doug, Boz, Bailey, and Vinnie hurried along the path, with the elf leading the way.

"Sarge, how far is a league?" Bailey asked.

"Depends. It could be anywhere from a mile and a half to three miles," Doug answered. "No matter what, we have a long walk ahead of us."

Chapter XVI

Deep inside the forest, the King's men, led by Captain Bedwell, uncovered a most fragile secret. He finally discovered Audra's sanctuary. Out of anger, his men violated, abused, carelessly and capriciously, everything in their sight that might have given comfort and security to anyone who'd lived there.

The bloodhounds took all day to lead the knaves, knights, and soldiers to the cave complex around the large clearing, with the fire pit in the center. The dogs went over the area, sniffing and howling. The land revealed evidence of the presence of many women.

The elder knight guessed they'd discovered the young girls' hiding place, the old witch, and perhaps the princess. Further, the searchers found many trails and scents to follow. The knaves didn't know which scent trail to start the hounds along first. The eldest knight told every knave to pick a scent and follow it with his dog; he instructed a knight and a few soldiers to go with them each. Since they had eight dogs, he had them choose eight scent trails, which led west and headed out of the forest.

None of the dogs picked up on the scent trail heading northwest. The elder knight would send a soldier on horseback back to the castle to report their findings and send the other searchers to him at the caves for further assignments.

Additional soldiers and household cavalry assembled at the cave site in the evening. They set up camp and started early the following day. Without success, the knaves, bloodhounds, knights, and soldiers returned from their day searches. Captain Bedwell left at dusk to return to the castle and inform the King of his accomplishments.

The elder knight reminded the search parties why they searched for Audra and the girls, citing her as responsible for hiding the girls this time every year, during the October fortnight. Any thought of the prisoners quickly faded from his mind with this discovery, which, according to law, took precedence over everything else.

That same evening, Zenega regained his clarity. When he heard of the discovery of the hiding place of the young girls, he went to the turret atop his apartments. He summoned one of his flying specters, a gargoyle-like ogre with a whistling device that only the creatures could hear. Moments later, a winged apparition appeared and perched on the battlement mounted on a parapet extended from the turret.

Zenega had created a gargoyle-like creature called a namatar. It was a hideous-looking animal with large wings and a body the size of a large dog when it sat on its haunches. It had four short limbs with large, sharp talons for feet and hands. Its head resembled that of a serpent, with teeth resembling a tiger's and large, pointed ears resembling a bat's. Black, scaly skin covered its body.

Zenega petted its repugnant head, lovingly stroked its back, and scratched it under its left wing. He ordered the namatar scout to assemble a group of acolytes and hunt for the women, telling him their last-known location. Zenega told the namatar they should herd them toward the King's men when they found them.

He returned to his apartment quickly, feeling another bout of the madness subtly approaching. The namatar flew off to its mountain cave to assemble the others. Then, head to the southwest to look for the prey.

While the search parties slept at the encampment at midnight, about ten namatars flew overhead. They filled the moonlit sky with their repulsive forms. The flapping of their wings broke the silence and awakened the captain of the guard with their loud whooshes. It gave him a creepy feeling. He knew who or what flew above him and his men.

They made circles over the encamped humans, purposely instilling fear and discomfort with their presence overhead. Concern and fear tingled through the captain when he imagined those things above taking their wrath out on his men. The hounds and horses were unnerved and very restless.

Eventually, the knaves had to rise and calm the animals. The namatars continued to the northeast on their quest. For hours, they scoured the hills and valleys, sniffing the air for the scent of human females. They pierced the darkness with their catlike eyes, penetrating it like a laser probe.

Shortly before dawn, a namatar caught a human female's pleasant scent and signaled the others through its bat-like telepathic technique.

The others gathered immediately around their fellow scout. They sniffed the air and recognized the scents. They began a search of the area, flying circular patterns like vultures looking for a fresh kill.

Rushing through the thick foliage, the flapping of wings grew louder above. Audra tried to calm the girls despite the panic she saw in their youthful eyes. Nearly frightened to death and despair, overwhelming their emotions, Audra felt powerless to help them.

Rebecca went to the front of the group. She admonished her newfound friends to stop acting like babies and get some backbone and resolve. Equally invested in surviving this atrocity, she told them any attention they brought by their behavior affected everyone.

Audra had intended to take them to an alternate hiding place she'd saved for this occasion. When they'd started there, she had warned them they would have to travel a whole day farther into the woods, across streams and creeks, to disperse any scents or trails. She told Rebecca of an escape route that led away from this new place that, if needed, would lead them back to the valley on its west side.

Audra knew the namatars were above, searching for them. She felt their presence. And while Rebecca warned the girls to remain calm, they continued to stay in fear instead. She knew Zenega had sent the namatars, determined to have his way once and for all.

Three namatars broke away from the others; they went unnoticed by the rest. The three plunged through the treetops and flew around until they located the path. They picked up the spicier scent of the girls and followed it.

From a distance, an elf, through his mysterious means, spotted the namatars flying toward him. He ran toward the group of females, yelling a warning that namatars were coming. Horror gripped everyone.

Rebecca shouted, "Keep moving and stay together. You two," she said, pointing at two girls, "Help Audra and keep moving."

The three namatars closed the distance, motivated by the intense scent of fear and women. The cluster ran as fast as they could. Rebecca watched the girls fall over each other, scratching and clawing at the foliage to regain their balance.

Audra realized that the youth's inexperience and the desire to survive contributed to the group's inability to engage in teamwork and assist each other. Audra and the girls only traveled as fast as the elf who lit the path ahead of them. The namatars drew nearer. Audra knew doom awaited them if she didn't find a place to hide quickly. She saw Rebecca trying to keep the girls together, but they weren't listening.

Audra stopped. She lifted her cane and sent out a wave of air. The girls all stopped, frozen in place. She proceeded to the head of the group with her assistant's help. Audra stretched out her arms and whispered a quick spell to control the girls' anxiety. Then she tapped her cane on the ground, and they woke up.

Rebecca prodded her friends to continue. The sound of the approaching namatars made Audra realize she had no time left. She called for the girls to pick quickly clovers and wildflowers, find a hiding place, and cover themselves. The girls responded quickly. Audra hid behind a tree and brought her cane up to her chest as her elf turned off his light.

The other namatars had experienced great difficulty focusing on the human scent. The dawn was nearly upon them, their time cut short. They knew they must return to their lair before the sun rose; otherwise, the burning rays would destroy them.

They made one last pass where they incorrectly suspected the human women might have hidden and headed northeast. Providence prevailed; the namatars searched at least a mile or more from where the girls lay hidden and never knew their three companions' fate.

Audra felt the renegade namatars come in low and slow, sniffing the air over the hiding places. She watched them circle carefully and then move on. She saw one turn back, dive into a large brush, and pluck out an object with its talons.

Fraught with abject terror, Rebecca and the girls collectively held their breath as the namatar rose with a faun in its grip. Finding that the being was not a human, the namatar dropped it. The faun scampered off. Audra saw the other two namatars return. She watched them drop lower and sniff every shrub.

She knew their instincts told them their prey was here. One girl tried to squelch another's cry, but the namatars heard it and raced to her spot. One dove into the shrub, grabbed her by the shoulders, and pulled her out.

She screamed a death scream that would curdle a woodsman's blood. The namatar raised her into the air and bellowed a victory growl, baring his nasty fangs and tickling her chin with his forked tongue. The other two joined him to watch as he was about to tear out the girl's throat.

Audra came out from behind the tree. A namatar, seeing her, bared his fangs and crouched to attack. Audra pointed her cane to her left toward the trees and spread their branches when he leaped. In that second, a ray of sunlight caught the namatar's head in mid-leap, and the creature disintegrated.

Sunlight struck the namatar, holding the girl at the same instant and suffering the same fate. The girl fainted, dropping to the ground. The third namatar tried to find a dark place to hide, but Audra dispatched him in the same manner before he could do so.

The girls came out of their hiding places, crying hysterically. Audra and Rebecca spoke to them soothingly, with reassuring words to quell their fears, but it was no help. She quickly encouraged the girls to move along the path to a nearby safe place she spoke about that was not far away.

Audra sequestered the girls under an umbrella of thick foliage, large enough to hide twice their number. It opened to a narrow passage, invisible even to a passing woodsman without previous knowledge. The heavy aromas from vines, wildflowers, and herbs masked the girls' presence.

Audra told the girls she expected the namatars to return the following evening. She needed to move everyone away from this place. Audra asked the girls to gather herbs and flowers with powerful scents that could break up their human ones when noonday came. She gathered all her strength and stood.

She explained to the girls why they must leave now and told them they must keep themselves covered with flowers and potent herbs. They traveled to avoid leaving any trails for hounds or namatars to follow.

Rebecca asked another girl to help her bring Audra along the path as they embarked on another arduous trek through the forest, searching for shelter and safety. Audra told Rebecca to head northwest along a little-known trail she had discovered many years earlier.

She felt tempted to seek guidance through her sorcery, but feared the advice she might perceive. There was not much she could do if it told of the danger. Instead, she sought guidance for safety.

The readings showed that heading northwest provided the best path. Audra thought of changing the girls into mice or birds, but they'd become vulnerable to another predator. She'd never forgive herself if any harm came to her charges, so she left well enough alone.

Audra thought perhaps they might reunite with those young men who'd helped the princess, who were now on their way to retrieve their iron war beast. She cackled under her breath, thinking about the iron beast spitting death from its nose at the namatars and causing Zenega further rage and torment.

Audra continued her exodus, taking the girls through the back trails and along streams and creeks only she knew. She made a concerted attempt to keep them concealed from any overhead prey. Arriving at a crossroads, Audra took the right fork on the trail instead of the left, believing the right path led to the valley's west side. She was always fearful that her age and complications from the spell she was under caused confusion, memory loss, and problems with her judgment.

Rebecca kept close to the witch. She felt an affinity toward Audra and a need to protect her. Most other girls felt the same devotion, but only a few joined Rebecca. Throughout their trek, Rebecca told everyone that she wanted no one to expose her as the princess if they got caught.

She intended to meet the same fate everyone else did. She felt they'd built a sisterhood among themselves and intended to survive. A while later, Audra saw an inviting clearing. She knew the girls felt exhausted from walking, so she told them to pick spots and lie down to nap.

Captain Linden, who was on the evening shift of knaves, hounds, and soldiers, straggled back toward the castle along a shortcut. He left the cave complex after the day shift, relieved him. As Linden passed a wall of shrubs, he heard the hounds become excited. He saw them drag their handlers into the shrubs.

The captain dismounted from his horse and followed. To his amazement, he saw the missing girls and Audra, the witch, fast asleep. The knaves hollered to the others to come quickly. The hound dogs, rudely barking and snarling, provoked surprise in Audra and the girls. The captain ordered the soldiers to surround them so they couldn't escape. Audra saw the girls huddle together, terrified and crying hysterically, fearing for their lives.

"Now we've got all of ye, and it will be the dungeons for ye until the King decides what's to be yer fate," a knight said.

Captain Linden sent a messenger to the remaining searchers at the encampment. He wanted to alert them he'd found the girls and that everyone should pack up and report to him. He'd need them to help take the women back to the castle. The day shift of guards, hounds, knaves, and knights arrived quickly.

The captain ordered them to herd the women together and march them along the trail back toward the castle. The senior knight ordered one knight to drag Audra along the path in chains. While trussing the witch up, the senior knight told her she'd burn at the stake for this outrage.

The same senior knight, who looked like the King of clubs, promised her the King would show no mercy toward her. When Rebecca heard this, she jumped into the knight's face and screamed furiously.

"You dare harm one hair on this woman's head, and I'll see that you get drawn and quartered, you impudent maniac."

"And who might yer be, ya little wildcat?" The knight asked, amused by this outburst.

Forgetting that she had planned to remain anonymous and driven by rage, she exclaimed, "I'm the Princess Rebecca, heir to the throne, you idiot. And I demand . . .no, I order you . . .to release every one of these girls right now!"

The knight merely stood there speechless with his mouth agape. He knew the princess had reportedly run away a few days ago, and the King had immediately sent out a search for her. But she wouldn't be here, not with this many peasant girls! She wouldn't have thrown in with them, he thought. He called for Captain Linden. When he arrived, the knight asked if he recognized this girl, pointing to Rebecca.

"She says she's Princess Rebecca."
The captain stared, his eyebrows arched, and his mouth opened in horror at the recognition while the color drained from the knight's face.

"Princess, do you realize how worried your parents are, and for the past few days . . . " he started admonishingly. Rebecca cut him off with another tirade.

"How dare you speak to me condescendingly, you baboon! I want these girls released and the witch Audra returned now!" She yelled loudly.

"See here, princess, you're in no position to dictate anything regarding the witch or these girls . . . king's orders. You're going home to the castle, and if you don't behave, I'll have to have you restrained."

"You dare threaten me, you moron; I'll have your gonads cut off. I'll have . . ."

"Here, you men," Captain Linden said, summoning some soldiers. "Restrain this girl and don't pay any attention to her ranting; she's gone loony. And don't let her mingle with the others or let her out of your sight. Otherwise, it'll be your heads!" He looked at the knight and asked, "What was the count of the girls, not including the princess and the witch?"

"Twenty-eight."

"Thank you," the captain said, and he walked off.

He then called a horseman to take immediately the princess back to the castle on horseback. Before the horseman could do so, she flew into a rage and insisted on traveling with the other girls. When the captain attempted to intervene and grab her, she invoked her authority as princess and heir to the throne.

She reminded him she'd become of age when she'd turned fourteen. Thus, the law forbade anyone outside the royal family from touching her without her permission, on penalty of death. The captain backed off and let her alone.

With great relief, the captain and his cavalcade finally reached the castle two hours later. The King and queen came outside the castle walls to greet and thank those who had worked so hard to retrieve their daughter. Word of her discovery and the others' capture had preceded them via a messenger sent by the senior knight.

The captain released the princess to the queen while the rest of the men ushered the girls to the dungeon rooms. When the queen took hold of Rebecca's left arm, Rebecca immediately and defiantly pulled away from her mother.

"Don't touch me, Mother," she said in an alarmingly strident tone. "If you think I'm going to allow any harm to come to these peasant girls, you've got another thing coming."

"Rebecca, that is none of your concern," the King said, walking behind them.

"That's what you think, Father. You don't know how much hate I have for what is being and has become allowable to go on here. I know everything, and I will stop it," she said triumphantly.

"Rebecca, go to your room and get a bath . . . and don't think you can sneak out again. I had the secret passage disabled. Yes, I found it, too. Did you think we adults didn't know about those passages?" The queen said smugly.

Rebecca gave her mother a look cold enough to form an iceberg, causing a mild tremble in the queen. She quickly marched off to her room for a well-needed bath. Her bath chamber resembled a Roman-style room with marble tiles on the floor and walls. It measured about the size of her bed-chamber . . . roomy but not excessive.

The bath was about three feet deep in the middle and contained several carved benches with headrests to relax on. She'd dismissed her attendants because she wanted to be alone, to think.

While soaking in the lilac-scented bubble bath, she thought of Vinnie and his friends. Rebecca wondered where they were and what they were doing. She thought about how much she missed Vinnie and wished he was sitting in the bubble bath with her. She stared at the ceiling with a shameless grin on her face.

Chapter XVII

Doug and the crew followed the elf through the forest all night. When the wee hours came, Doug suggested they stop and get some sleep and then continue. By dawn, the elf had taken them to the forest's edge and the road. He told them he couldn't go any further; otherwise, he'd lose his powers and become vulnerable to the King's men.

He directed the men to the left, where he said the hut and their iron beast were waiting for them; the castle was back to the right. Bailey immediately recognized the road from a fallen maple tree he'd noticed when they had passed that way the day before. It meant Vicky's hiding place was about five miles to the west.

While saying thank you to the elf, Doug heard galloping horses and immediately warned the men to take cover. Then, he dove into the forest and hid under the thick foliage. A moment later, a dozen mounted soldiers rode past them. Doug noticed they headed toward, not away from, the castle.

"Christ, that was close," Boz said, slightly shaken.

"Yeah, we'd better keep our wits about us, so we don't get caught out in the open," Doug said. "We'll parallel the road through the forest to hide if we hear more horsemen. All right, c'mon, let's get moving."

Doug kept the men close to the edge of the tree line until they came to the end of the forest. Then, they faced the problem of open terrain, sparser trees, and a lack of foliage that would not conceal them. Around noon, Doug and the crew approached the area of the old hut where the knights captured them. He told the men to stay low and sneak around if any knights or soldiers lurked nearby before going to the tank.

Once he became satisfied no one was in sight, Doug ran for the cover of the thick foliage behind the hut, followed by the crew, who quickly cleared away the debris that had fallen on Vicky. Doug observed how well the trees concealed her.

He couldn't believe no one had discovered her or even guessed something this big could hide under the fallen branches. He ordered everyone to get in the tank. After the crew cleared the hatches, a slight tremor reverberated through Vicky.

"Did you feel that?" Bailey asked.

"Yeah, and I thought I heard something, too . . like a growl or a metallic groan," Vinnie added.

"Ya know, I thought I heard something like that the day we left her," Boz said.

"Okay, men, let's get our asses inside and crank her up. We have a score to settle," with determination he said, "now isn't the time to let our imaginations run away with our sanity," Doug said.

Doug and the crew went through their start-up checks, and Vinnie cranked her up. Vicky's big engine came to life with no hesitation.

"Everyone, arm yourselves with the small arms you brought along, and the issued CAR-15s, and make sure they're locked and loaded," Doug ordered.

The crew put on their holsters, stuck their Colt Model 1911 .45 semiautomatic pistols inside them, and then slung their 5.56-millimeter CAR-15 carbines over their shoulders. Doug refused to carry the army-issue 9-millimeter Beretta M9 because, in his opinion, it couldn't stop a pissant.

"Next time anyone wants to take us prisoner, they'll be in for a real ass-whuppin!" Boz said.

Doug snickered as each crew member added his version of the same thought. Vinnie pulled Vicky out from behind the hut and turned east along the road. Debris falling off the tank and grinding under her tracks made a loud racket. Doug swung the turret, so it faced forward.

He ordered the men to charge all their weapons and the .50 and CO-AX (Co-axial) .30. The crewmen opened the hatches and stuck their heads out, looking for someone or something to vent their wrath. As Vinnie drove, Doug remembered that the road turned left and went into the valley and the castle at the crest. He told Vinnie to turn right at that point and find a clearing.

Vinnie complied and found a clearing not fifty feet in the forest among some low shrubbery, ground into a pulp as the tank drove over it. He turned the tank to face the road from which they came, and Boz aimed the main gun toward the opening. Doug told Vinnie to keep the engine idling.

"Okay, everyone, out of your hatches . . . but stay on top of the tank if we have trouble. I want someone on a machine gun at all times. The rest of you, keep your small arms close," Doug cautioned. "What do you suggest we do to help these people?"

"Hey, look," Bailey said, pointing toward the ground. "Looks like a big fight happened here, judging by all the footprints and broken bushes."

"Okay, Vinnie, you man the fifty cal. while the rest of us investigate," Doug ordered.

Doug jumped off the tank with his sidearm and looked around the ground at the broken branches and twigs.

"Sarge, look, dog poop," Boz said, pointing. "Those hounds must have been here and found something."

"Or someone, or a group of someones," Boz interjected.

"Yeah, there seem to be a lot of paws, foot, and hoof prints here," Doug said, thinking out loud.

"Hey, look over here!" Bailey yelled from the trail on the other side of the clearing. "Footprints are heading north. They seem to go toward the road we were just on."

"Sarge, over there on that tree . . . what is that?" Vinnie asked, pointing to a tree behind the tank.

"It seems to be a woman's shawl," Doug said.

"Well, that settles it. The girls got caught and taken to the castle," Bailey said, disappointed.

An elf jumped out of nowhere and onto the tank's turret. The elf danced around, made funny incantations, and giggled like a drunk. No one recognized him as one of the other elves they'd met.

"Who are you, little fellow?" Vinnie asked as the rest of the crew remounted Vicky.

"I'm Jambor," the elf said, dancing around.

"Why are you here?" Doug asked.

"They're coming for the girls with many swirls and a-flying they'll a-be. The namatars will whisk them away while the sorcerer plays away, and soon merry he will be," intoned the elf.

"When are these . . .namatars . . Coming?" Doug pressed. "Can you tell us what happened here?" Boz asked.

"No, he can't," said another voice from the trees.

The men drew their weapons and took a defensive stance, aiming at the trees behind them and expecting an attack. Vinnie turned the cupola around and aimed the .50 into the woods. Then Doug saw a man walk out from behind a giant redwood tree. His attire suggested that he was a woodsman and looked ancient, with a long, white beard and white hair. He carried a wooden cane from a tree branch and wore an alpine-style cap.

"It is not important to tell you my name. I have lived in the forest all my life. If that satisfies your curiosity, I am the guardian of the trees, the animals, and nature," he said.

"When Audra first came to me, I nursed her back to health. You see, the sorcerer Zenega was very cruel to her. He cast her away from the castle. He cast a spell on her, leaving her as she is now for the rest of her life . . . until someone or something breaks the spell." He walked to Vicky and placed his hand on the drive sprocket. "She speaks to me . . .your Vicky does. She says she loves all of you and is proud of your actions. What? Oh yes, she says she loves her name, too."

"Hey, old-timer," Vinnie said, "what are you trying to pull? Vicky is fifty-two tons of humping, homogenous steel. This iron lady can't talk . . . ."

The woodsman interrupted. "Vicky says, 'Vinnie, shut up and listen for a change. If you did that with Angela, you might get along better.'"

Doug, Boz, and Bailey plopped on their butts, mouths agape, and shock on their faces, not knowing what to do or say next.

"Geeeez, where in the hell are we?" Boz whispered.

"There is no way that old man could know about Vinnie and Angela or that we named this tank Vicky," Bailey said in a cautious tone, leaning toward Doug.

"Are you trying to convince us that this tank is alive, old man?" Doug declared as he climbed off the tank.

"Oh no. But your Vicky speaks to me, that I know," the old man said, running his fingers along the exhaust grates. "She wants to know when we will fight and free the girls and the princess."

"Hell, you tell us?" Bailey quipped.

"Look, old timer, we're figuring out where we go next and what we're supposed to do. We don't know the fate of those women, much less what or who we're supposed to fight. If you can fill us in on what the Sam Hill is going on instead of giving us this yarn that our tank's become bewitched and speaks to you, we'd be mighty grateful," Doug orated with a southern drawl.

Vicky lurched forward and stopped abruptly, causing Boz and Bailey to fall off the tank and onto the ground and Vinnie to fall off the commander's hatch and onto the floor. "Heeeeey!" The others heard Vinnie cry from inside the tank.

"Well, sarge, I guess the iron lady hath spoken, and I doth believe she's bewitched," Bailey moaned while he tried to get off the ground.

"She certainly has our attention now, doesn't she?" Doug added.

Bailey and Boz brushed themselves off and regained their composure as Vinnie jumped out of the commander's hatch and climbed to the ground.

"What was that all about?" Vinnie squeaked.

The old man put his hand back on the drive sprocket for a moment and whispered against the track. After a few moments, he came away from the tank.

"Vicky said to tell you she was sorry if you were frightened, but she needed your full and undivided attention. She says Audra cast a spell on her. The spell has temporarily empowered her to be an instrument in destroying the evil sorcerer Zenega.

"Vicky says that, along with her crew, Audra is prepared to do battle against the namatars and Zenega. She desires to free the girls and bring peace and tranquility back to the Kingdom," the old man informed them.

"To do that, we have to know what happened and where everyone is, and then we'll make a plan," Doug insisted.

The old man recounted the events that had taken place since the men left the cave complex to get Vicky.

"The King's search parties discovered the women, Audra, and the princess, here in this clearing. The king has imprisoned the girls and

Audra inside the dungeons, awaiting Zenega's pleasure.

"Audra sits in a cell by herself, awaiting execution. They'll do it because she harbored the girls and the princess. What is unknown is when Zenega will begin selecting girls and committing his hideous acts," the old man concluded.

"How do you know all of this?" Doug asked the old man curiously.

"Audra has communicated with me. I feel her presence and her pain."

"Why don't we go to the castle and begin blasting?" Vinnie suggested.

"Yeah, good idea, Vinnie," Bailey interjected sarcastically. "Why don't we do that . . just bring that castle crumbling down on everybody and crush the good with the evil and end up killing all those cute girls, Audra, and the princess . . .hmm?"

"We need to find the girls first, get them out of there, and then start blasting," Vinnie corrected Bailey.

"All right, we go in tonight, armed to the teeth. We'll break them out . . . quietly . . . get them a safe distance away from the castle, and then have it out with this Zenega," thought Doug aloud.

"Old man, can you tell us what we face inside the castle? Is there a way to get back inside without being discovered? How many soldiers, guards, knights, and people like that are there?"

The old man explained to them the troop disposition within the castle.

"Zenega has his bodyguard detachment. They wear red uniforms, and their sole purpose is to defend the person of the sorcerer. Some believe they are namatars in human form. They live on the top floors of the sorcerer's residence," he warned them.

"We've met those guys, and I have a special interest in meeting them again . . only on my terms this time!" Vinnie said with hate in his voice.

The old man drew a map in the dirt. He outlined a trail on the valley's west side, which ran north to a clearing intersecting with the east-west road. The road went east to the main north-south road near the castle.

"You must return the way you came," he said, pointing west, "until you see a wooden candy cane-colored stake by a pine tree. It is the only one. You must then go through the shrubbery and get onto the trail. It is a long journey to that intersection, but you can't miss it because Vicky will find it. Then enter the castle as you escaped," the old man cautioned.

Doug thanked the old man and climbed back onto the tank. The rest of the crew followed and took their stations.

"Good hunting," the old man called out.

Vinnie drove west along the road for a few miles until Vicky abruptly stopped. Her turret turned right, and she pointed her main gun toward some bushes. Vinnie turned Vicky to the right and followed the main gun's direction. He mumbled to himself, telling Vicky to stop being over-controlling.

"Christ, she's truly bewitched," Doug chimed in when the turret spun to the right.

"I'm glad she's on our side," Bailey added.

After about fifty yards, Doug saw a short, wooden candy cane-colored stake extending from the ground before a wall of high bushes. Doug told Vinnie to drive the tank through the bushes. They came through the other side and found themselves in some dense forest. Fortunately for Doug, the trail seemed wide enough to accommodate the tank's width, measuring about fourteen feet.

When Vinnie reached the intersection, turned right, and continued, sundown was already approaching. He crossed a shallow, narrow river and drove out onto vast farmland, extending to the limits of their vision.

Vinnie drove until they reached the old, abandoned shacks that bore the scars of a hamlet or village that had once thrived there. Vinnie parked Vicky in a logical area to the left and shut her engine off. Doug climbed onto the top of the turret and stood on the hatch, looking through his binoculars.

He looked toward the castle to see if he could detect anything unusual or if search parties were still scouring the countryside looking for them. "I figure it's about a half-mile to the castle. We'll eat and rest until it's good and dark. Then we'll put on our commando faces and head out. I think Vicky'll be fine here, off the road in this cornfield," Doug said.

"Yeah, I'm starving. I can't remember when we ate last," Vinnie added.

"Who has an appetite at a time like this?" Bailey quipped.

Boz opened a package of MREs and gulped it down. Doug invoked light and sound discipline, which meant they could use no light. Nor make any sound from metal-on-metal contact if anyone who might recognize them wandered around the nearby area. After everyone had finished his meal, Doug went over the plan again.

"Let's review this once more. We intend to sneak along this road until we hit the main highway, cross it, find the stream the sewer system flows into, and return through it. Then, we try to make our way to a familiar location where we can reenter the castle. At last, we will rescue everyone and bring them back here where we can protect them."

The men prepared themselves. They donned their web belts, weapons, and KA-BAR survival knives. They checked their ammunition, ensured they had full canteens, and each had a flashlight.

"Does anyone have any ideas about how to darken our faces?" Doug asked.

Vinnie jumped onto the tank and looked through his duffel bag. He handed Doug a small Ziploc bag with several camouflage face paint sticks.

"Where did you get these?" Doug asked, surprised.

"Ya never know when you'll need 'em, so I just keep 'em just in case," Vinnie said proudly.

The others merely shook their heads in amazement. After applying the paint to their faces, they headed toward the castle.

Chapter XVIII

Rebecca, frustrated and angry, was pacing back and forth in her room when the door opened, and her mother entered.

"It's time for supper. Your father expects you to attend to him in the dining room," she said forcefully.

"I'm not hungry, Mother," she replied arrogantly.

"Rebecca! You will attend to your father, or I will have you dragged down to the dining room by the guard like a peasant girl and humiliate you. Do you understand? I will no longer tolerate this insolent behavior; do you hear me, young lady?" said the queen, raising her voice.

The princess ignored her mother and walked out the door toward the first floor's dining room. When she arrived, she took her seat but did not speak with or look at her father. She ignored him and dug into her food without waiting for anyone else to start. This invidious act of forgetting her manners disturbed the King mightily, but he said nothing to his only daughter. He knew she had him wrapped tightly around her little finger.

The queen arrived a moment later and sat at the table. While she placed her napkin on her lap, she noticed the undignified manner Rebecca ate her food.

"That's very rude, Rebecca," she said. Rebecca ignored her mother and kept eating.

"Alex! Say something to your daughter."

"Ann, just let her be. You've both had a trying day today. Any further animosity would be unproductive. After a good night's rest, we will feel better in the morning," suggested the King.

Rebecca finished supper and rose from her chair to leave the dining room.

"Where are you going?" The queen demanded.

"For a walk," the princess said.

"I forbid it," the queen responded, raising her voice.

Rebecca ignored her and departed. The queen threw her napkin on the table and rose, but the King grabbed her wrist.

"Sit down, Ann; she's just furious right now and needs to think about her transgressions and how she will atone for them. After all, she has embarrassed herself and the court," the King said.

"Alex, you are a fool or very naïve if you think that girl," . . . she pointed toward the doorway . . . "has no intention of atoning for what she did. Rebecca is rebellious and belligerent, and I doubt her anger will subside soon. She's discovered the secret of the October fortnight and disapproves intently. She is determined to stop it, and you know Lord Zenega. He will not be too understanding of her attempts to thwart his practices," the queen huffed into his face, her green-blue eyes bulging.

"He might even harm her . . . and that worries me, even if it doesn't you."

Rebecca walked outside into the cool air. The palace guards knew they should stay alert and watch the princess if she wandered the castle grounds. They had the King's proclamation to detain her if she misbehaved or tried to leave the castle. Taking precautions, the King had ordered his captain of the guard to double the sentries precisely for that purpose.

Deep in thought, Rebecca knew she needed to save her newfound friends and Audra from the eventual fate she knew awaited them. If only she could figure out how to get to or find Vinnie and his friends, they'd know what to do.

Darkness fell upon the land. Rebecca thought those namatars flying around trying to find young girls would soon take to the sky again. She remembered when Audra had told the girls about the namatars. The thought of the frightful experience she'd had in the forest with them sent a chill through her, and she went back inside the castle's living quarters.

She thought about returning to her room, but an inspiration crossed her heart. She wanted to visit Audra and the girls and give them hope. Rebecca searched for and found the stairway leading to the dungeons and cautiously descended the steps.

When she reached the landing, she noticed the first pod of cells was empty. She knew that meant the girls were most likely on the east or west end of the dungeon complex. She tried the east end first, since it was nearer the dungeon dining room.

While she walked along the corridors, Rebecca found nooks she thought she'd use as hiding places when the guards and jailers came by.

She knew that if the guards found her here, they'd take her immediately to the captain of the guard and then to her parents.

She finally reached the last pod of cells and saw the girls in the first and Audra in the remaining one. Rebecca noticed the pods had become arranged in a semicircle with six cells in a pod. She saw the big table in the room and noticed the grating under the table, which Vinnie had told her he and his friends had lifted to escape.

She saw neither the jailer nor a guard anywhere around. Rebecca sneaked to the first pod and surprised the girls. They expressed excitement to see her, and she responded equally to seeing them. They cried and babbled all at once, but Rebecca raised her hand and whispered to them to remain quiet lest the guards overhear them.

Even if falsely, she assured them she would figure out how to get them out. She told them they needed to remain hopeful and patient until then. Then she excused herself and hurried over to Audra's cell.

The old woman lay on her cot. She looked exhausted and ill. She told Rebecca, "My child, you are still in great danger from Zenega and must remain vigilant. Our friends are coming soon. It would be best if you were prepared to do whatever they say.

"There is a significant battle to be fought, which, if the strange men are victorious, will change the entire existence of this land and those who live within it. Peace will eventually prevail, but many will die to attain this peace.

"Go now, Rebecca. Leave the dungeons and go to your room to await your fate."

"But Audra, I have many questions to ask you," Rebecca implored.

"Mercy, princess . . . I'm too ill and too weak to speak any longer . . . please, leave and quickly before someone sees you," Audra pleaded hoarsely.

Tearfully, Rebecca said goodbye to everyone and hurried back to the stairs. She ascended to the first floor and then went to her room. Zenega drifted in and out of his spells of madness. When he felt coherent enough to think, he depended on his assistant, Melonjack, to handle his mundane tasks.

Melonjack, an apprentice but not a sorcerer, kept Zenega informed about the castle's things of interest. He had told Zenega when the hounds discovered the girls and when the soldiers had brought them and Audra to the dungeons. Zenega, immensely pleased, looked forward to satisfying his lust and exacting his revenge on Audra.

After midnight, he thought about which girl he would take to the caves and his hidden lair. His actual residence was his lair, protected by his small army of namatars. He, Zenega . . . the greatest sorcerer in the land . . . kept his secrets, potions, and serums. In his hidden lair, he did his dirtiest and most despicable work; that was where fulfilling their destinies awaited these girls.

Audra's fate lay with the King's proclamation. When he burned her at the stake for crimes against the realm, the King would leave some satisfaction for Zenega. The sorcerer intended to devastate the princess, who had formed such a fond friendship with the illustrious witch . . .a proper punishment for being an impudent girl. For now, Zenega only yearned to survive the evening.

He assigned his Red Guards to find and secure all escape routes into and out of the castle. This way, he could be sure that the strangers who had escaped had come on a quest. His Red Guards had prepared a greeting if they tried interfering with his plans.

Doug and the crew crossed the old north-south irrigation ditch to the right of the road and went a few yards into the crop fields before they cut north toward the castle. When they approached the tree line, he and the men took cover and scanned the river and the castle wall, particularly the mouth of the sewer they had escaped. Vinnie removed his small backpack and pulled out a pair of AN/PVS-5 night vision goggles.

"Vinnie, where the hell did you get those?" Doug whispered incredulously.

"They issued them to me last year while I was on annual training. The supply folks were giving them away," Vinnie said innocently. "I thought they might come in handy someday."

"Christ, Vinnie, sometimes you amaze even me," Bailey suggested.

"Okay, you men, quiet down. Vinnie, scan the area and tell me what you see," Doug ordered.

Vinnie scanned the front of the sewer entrance, then the area's right and left of the castle wall.

"Nothing, sarge. It's all clear."

"Listen up, men," Doug warned, concern in his voice. "Do not for one minute think you're invincible just because you have guns. These characters have crossbows, bows, and arrows and they're well versed in using them. Those weapons are as deadly as if they had guns. They can engage you from a distance, just as you can them. Don't get complacent. Okay, let's go. Stay together."

Doug crossed the river and went up the incline to the mouth of the sewer. The men removed their flashlights and searched the sewer while entering the dark cavern. After a few yards, Boz spotted a flight of narrow stairs leading to some unknown place.

"Hey, sarge," he whispered loudly, "look at this. A flight of stairs." The others came over to see what Boz had found.

"Go up and see where it goes. There's probably a door somewhere," Doug said.

Boz ascended the stairs until he came to a landing. There, to his right, he saw a small half-door. He first pulled on it, and then he pushed. The door creaked open. Boz shone his flashlight into the darkness and saw the passage.

"Hey, sarge," Boz yelled in a whisper. "Here's a door that leads to a passage."

They ascended the stairs.

"I bet this is the way Rebecca said she got out. See, it's left unlocked," offered Vinnie. "I bet it leads to her room. If it does, we can at least get her out."

"How will you identify which room is hers without waltzing into the wrong one and causing pandemonium?" Doug asked.

"Rebecca told me she had scratched a big R on the wall with a stone before leaving, so she had a way to find her room in case she needed to," Vinnie offered.

"Boy, you two got to know each other, didn't you?" Bailey teased.

"Well, I . . ."

"All right, listen up," Doug admonished. "Vinnie, you and Bailey go through the door and see if you can first find a way inside the castle and then if you can find Rebecca. If you succeed, one of you will come and find us, and we'll return. And if we find a way in, I'll send Boz to get you."

Vinnie and Bailey entered the passageway. Doug and Boz descended the stairs and followed the sewer deeper into the castle's bowels.

"It's darker than a coal mine in here," Vinnie whispered.

"Look," Bailey said, shining his flashlight on the cracks in the walls as they walked, outlining the locations of the secret doors.

Finally, they reached a door where Vinnie saw the big R on the wall and the outline of Rebecca's door. Bailey saw the chain and handle to his left and the broken chain on the right.

"Can you hear anything, Vinnie?"

"You're kidding, right?" Vinnie asked, unamused.

"Look for a peephole or something."

"Ya know, this wall is hot like there's a fire on the other side," Bailey said, looking closely at the small, square stone blocks in the center of the wall door.

"Look, one of these blocks is loose. Hold my flashlight while I work it free with my knife."

The small block slid out after a few minutes of Bailey using the knife on it. They turned off their flashlights and peeked into the room. There, they saw Rebecca pacing back and forth. She wore her golden hair down, covering her shoulders. She had on a purple and white dress. They saw no one else in the room with her.

"Psssssst, Rebecca!" Vinnie whispered loudly, holding his flashlight under his chin. Rebecca stopped dead in her tracks, her eyes widening into large pools of blue and white. She turned her head toward the hearth. Rebecca barely saw the missing block, and the illuminated face. She moved toward the hearth.

"Vinnie, is that you?" She whispered back excitedly.

"Yeah, it's Bailey and me. Are you alone?"

"Yes . . . yes, I am," she said excitedly.

"Okay, stand back," he warned.

Bailey grabbed the handle and pulled it with all his strength; the block wall door gave way and rotated ninety degrees on a shaft in its center. Vinnie walked into Rebecca's room. Before he got to take in all the frills and things, Rebecca jumped into his arms and showered his face with kisses and a bear hug. She got camo paint all over her face.

She gave Bailey a hug and a light kiss, too. Then she put her right index finger to her lips to warn them they should stay quiet. Rebecca quietly warned them that Zenega had ears in the walls and motioned for them to return to the passageway.

"Oh, Vinnie, I wished you'd find me so hard and rescue the girls and me! How did you find me? I have so many questions."

"Rebecca put a sock in it for a minute. Listen, we must get you and everyone else out of this place. Doug and Boz are looking for a way into the dungeon room through the sewer.

"We found this passageway and came for you. Change your clothes, and let's get the hell out of here," Vinnie told her, "And wipe off your face!"

"Vinnie, what does it mean to . . . put a sock in it?" Rebecca asked,

174

somewhat annoyed at his choice of words. She suspected that whatever he'd said wasn't nice.

"Rebecca, all Vinnie meant was that we are so excited to see you, but we don't want to draw any attention to you or ourselves. We need to get out of here and talk later," Bailey said, trying to save Vinnie.

"I'll be right back. Don't go anywhere without me," Rebecca ordered. Then she turned on her heel and hurried off to change clothes.

"What's beyond this corridor, I wonder?" Vinnie mused.

"Don't know. Let's check it out while Rebecca changes," Bailey said.

Vinnie and Bailey walked a few yards along the dark corridor and came to a T intersection. Bailey took out his compass and saw they headed east, meaning the rest of the castle and the sorcerer's residences were probably to the left along the north corridor.

The two men returned to Rebecca's door as she exited her room. She had worn her riding pants and boots again, but she'd brought a warmer coat with her this time. She'd tied her hair into a ponytail. Vinnie and Bailey shut the wall door, and Bailey replaced the small block.

"Rebecca, have you ever explored the passageway in this direction?" Bailey asked, pointing east.

"No, I haven't. Why?"

"We think it leads to Zenega's place, and we need to find out. You go back down to the sewer and go to the right and see . . ."

"I'm going with you! Don't argue with me."

"Rebecca, it's too dang . . ."

"I don't care, Vinnie! I'm going with you, and that's final, so let's move," she confidently said.

"The princess has spoken," Bailey chimed.

"What sorcery is in your hand that can cast a light without a fire?" She asked.

"It's called a flashlight. Please don't ask more questions; it would take too long to explain, and we don't have the time now," Vinnie told her.

Vinnie led the trio to the left at the intersection. He took them along a long passageway and down a long, steep flight of stairs to a landing. He felt cool air blowing through the walls when he crossed the landing.

"We are crossing above the rear gate to the castle, which leads to the knight's village," Rebecca said when she looked out from between the wide spaces in the wall.

Then he took them up another long, steep flight of stairs, arrived at a floor that extended a few yards and turned left into a straight passageway. As Vinnie passed through the long corridor, he noticed a peephole in each outlined room.

The three listened and spied through the holes into the rooms, which seemed to have no occupants. At the last door, the trio stopped again. Vinnie and Bailey turned off their flashlights and looked inside.

"Who is that?" Bailey asked Rebecca, moving away from the door so she could look.

"That's Zenega," she whispered, terrified, "and his apprentice, Melonjack."

Vinnie listened at the hole and heard the two speaking.

"A namatar has just brought word, my lord," Melonjack said. "Your consort awaits your arrival with the first host. She is prepared and anxious."

"Yes, many hosts will go to the location of my darling bride, where she will fulfill her annual ovumentation ritual. Her ovaries are overabundant and in need of release . . . as am I. Then, the madness will be gone for another year. I will complete the process by fertilizing the hosts. Then, in a month, new namatars will emerge from their bodies. Those who survive the birthing process will prevail," Zenega revealed.

"But why must the host be so young a girl?" The novice Melonjack inquired.

"Because in their youth, while they mature, there is something that enhances the incubation of the namatars; adult women over eighteen no longer possess it," Zenega explained.

Vinnie could only imagine the look on Bailey's face as he heard this, but he guessed it expressed the same shock he did. He grabbed Bailey and Rebecca, turned his flashlight on dim, and hurried away with the two right behind him.

When the passageway ended, he took another left turn, and they all climbed another long flight of stairs. Vinnie felt too scared to say anything. He needed to find the sarge and inform him of their uncovered horror.

He led the way across another breezy corridor on the landing, guessing it was the castle's front gate. Then, down another long flight of stairs and a landing, they came upon a dead end.

"I can't believe I heard that," Vinnie puffed, out of breath.

"It's the most disgusting thing I've ever known anyone to do to a girl; it reminds me of the movie Alien when the thing comes out of that guy's chest; remember that?" Bailey puffed, also out of breath.

"I'm not sure I understand what Zenega was talking about," Rebecca said innocently, "but it sounded gruesome and disgusting if I heard correctly."

"Becky, honey, you don't even want to know what they were talking about, but I will explain later when we hook up with the sarge. So how do we get through this wall?" Vinnie asked, confused.

"Look. See these indentations in each brick that outline this wall? They're about the size of a fist. Start pulling on them and see what happens," Bailey suggested.

A moment later, when Rebecca pulled on a particular brick, the wall pivoted on its center shaft. It revealed the same landing that led to the door to the original passageway. It nearly scared the life out of Boz, who was coming up the stairs at that moment.

"Where the hell have you guys been? Sarge's become pissed and wants all of us to regroup with him now . . . oh hi, Rebecca . . . so let's go," Boz said hurriedly.

"You'll never believe what we found out! Where is sarge, anyway? Did you guys find a way into the castle?" Bailey asked excitedly.

"We're still looking." He responded.

Boz led the four sloshing along the sewer toward where Doug waited. Rebecca held Vinnie's hand again while they walked. After Boz had traveled a few yards, he came to the intersection and turned left. He continued farther into the dark sewer tunnel until they found Doug sitting under a set of handholds leading to an overhead grating.

Boz and Doug had scouted the sewer earlier and had discovered that it had an exit somewhere. There wasn't any noticeable human traffic within the dungeon complex, either.

"It's about time you two got back! What took you so long?" Doug asked, exasperated. "Do you realize what time it is?"

"Yeah, sarge, we know, but we had to get the princess, and then we overheard that sorcerer talking," Vinnie said.

He explained what he overheard and why Doug needed to get Audra and the girls away from the castle and safety before midnight. When the realization of the full impact of Zenega's atrocities hit Rebecca, she cried hysterically and screamed, "No, no, no, it can't be!" Until Vinnie grabbed her and shoved her face into his chest, reminding her they'd get discovered if she didn't stay quiet.

"We need a plan then, to get everyone out . . . and quickly," Doug urged.

"We don't even know where they're confined," Vinnie said.

"I do; they're on the east end of the first floor of the dungeons," Rebecca replied between sobs.

"I don't suppose you know how to get through those secret passages?" Vinnie asked inquisitively.

"I saw something along a wall that looked like a corridor. I think it was in the cellar, but I'm not sure," Rebecca said.

"Why don't we just head east along this sewer and see if we can find a grate?" Bailey suggested.

Doug thought for a moment. "Vinnie, you and Rebecca go check out that location she just told us about and then come back to where we are. Do nothing on your own, understand?"

"Okay, sarge. Let's go, Becky," Vinnie said, taking Rebecca's hand

and heading back along the sewer.

Doug took the rest of the group, heading east along the sewer and continuing in that direction from the intersection. While he trekked along, he looked for signs of ladders, handholds or openings leading to the dungeons. Meanwhile, Rebecca and Vinnie reentered the passageway she had first escaped and searched for the spot Rebecca had seen before.

While the two looked, Vinnie noticed the outline of another wall door. He turned off his flashlight and looked for the slightest sign of a light source. When he found it, he set his flashlight to dim.

"Is this what you saw?" He asked Rebecca and moved away from the spot.

"I think so," she whispered; with her face so close to his, he could smell the freshness in her hair. It caused a stir in him.

She took Vinnie's face in both hands on a whim and kissed him passionately.

"Rebecca!" He hissed loudly. "Are you crazy? We don't have time for romance. "Stop this nonsense," he whispered in exasperation, diminishing his momentary passion.

"I love you, Vinnie," she exclaimed.

"Becky, honey, don't start. Not now. We can talk about it later. Right now, we've got work to do," he said, calming down. "Let's start looking for a way to open this wall."

They searched around the wall and the door's outline but found nothing. Off to the right, Rebecca felt a stone protrusion. It was high, and she could barely reach it . . . the vertical stone measured about a foot tall and three inches wide and extended about four inches.

She showed Vinnie what she'd found. Vinnie handed her the flashlight while he attempted to pull on the protrusion. The wall door popped open just enough to get his hands around the edge and pull it when he did so.

Excitedly, Vinnie opened the wall door just enough to stick his head through it and look up and down the corridor to check for guards or jailers. When he saw no one, he backed up and closed the wall door, reached up, and pushed the stone lever back in.

He then took out his compass and determined that the east end of the dungeons went to the right after entering the corridor. Vinnie estimated his proximity to the sewer and the end of the castle. He was more to the west of the sewer than the east. That meant it was a long way to the east end of the dungeons.

Vinnie also determined that no other secret passages existed on this level to the east side. That meant the sewers were the only other way through. He explained his theory to Rebecca, and she concurred with Vinnie's estimation.

Vinnie needed to decide if he should take a chance and risk having to confront the guards if discovered, possibly getting into a gunfight . . . or return to the sewers and Doug. Vinnie had his sidearm and CAR-15 slung over his back with ample ammunition.

However, the loud noise of gunfire in the narrow corridors would alert everyone in the castle that something terrible had happened in the cellars.

Chapter XIX

Have you seen Rebecca"?

"No, Ann. I've been sitting here reading since supper, right before you," the King replied.

"Well, I'm worried. Usually, Rebecca comes in and out of here with her friends, but they haven't even seen her since she returned," observed the queen.

"It's only been a day, Ann. What do you expect?" The King asked, expressing concern after what she went through and expecting her to be traumatized or worse.

"Alex, you're an idiot. She has you so wrapped around her little finger that it makes me jealous. That child has become spoiled and very headstrong; I'm going up to her room to check on her," the queen said, and she left.

The queen walked through Rebecca's unlocked door and found her daughter gone again. It was clear she'd changed her clothes. The queen saw her daughter's dress on the floor, and her drawers were open, showing that she'd fled.

The queen, irate, checked the secret passage doors' mechanism and felt satisfied her daughter couldn't have gotten out that way again. She returned to her apartments and zeroed in on the King.

Melonjack, eavesdropping at the bank of listening hoses that the sorcerer had built, overheard the King and queen's conversation regarding their daughter. He informed Zenega.

"Master, Rebecca is again afoot and is probably up to no good." When he heard that, Zenega ordered the captain of his Red Guards to send a detachment immediately to the dungeons to guard the women; he told Melonjack to send the signal for three namatars to come to the castle. Zenega chose three girls directly and immediately ordered them taken to the lair. He did not want to leave anything to chance or risk anyone interfering with his plans.

Doug and the rest of the crew located a grating close to the east dungeons. Doug asked Boz to keep a tab on foot traffic going to and from the area. So far, it remained light; he figured it wasn't anything more than a change of the guard detail. However, before he went any further, he planned to wait for Vinnie and Rebecca to return.

Meanwhile, Vinnie took a chance and went for it. He reopened the wall door, stepped into the corridor, with Rebecca following him, closed the door behind them, and headed east. While walking, he kept alert for places to hide if someone came from either direction.

He noticed a few corridors leading off the main one and a few doors. Vinnie checked them to make sure they were unlocked. After a few minutes, he heard footsteps coming and hid in a nook, wrapping around to a hidden staircase. Two jailers passed going west. When Vinnie thought it safe, he took Rebecca's hand and continued east.

When it seemed merely a few more feet before reaching the pod of cells, he heard more footsteps. They sounded louder this time, as if they were in marching order, and came from behind him. Rebecca pulled Vinnie into a nook she'd used before when she'd been there and concealed the two from the soldiers. As they passed, Rebecca visibly trembled.

"What's wrong?" Vinnie whispered.

"Red Guards," she said, sobbing. "Zenega has sent his Red Guards to watch the girls until he comes for them. What are we going to do now, Vinnie?"

"I guess it's game time," Vinnie said as he unslung his CAR-15 from around his back.

"What is that?" Rebecca asked, pointing to the rifle.

"You'll see in a minute. I wonder where Sarge and the others are?" He asked himself aloud.

Vinnie told Rebecca to stay behind him as they crept up on the Red Guards, who watched over the girls with four soldiers and a jailer. He switched his CAR-15 to Semi-auto and charged the bolt. Vinnie had never experienced the fear and anger he felt at that moment.

He'd never killed a human before, but he couldn't allow those girls to meet a fate so despicable and heinous . . . unjustifiable by any human standards. Vinnie knew what they were planning on doing was a total atrocity.

He steeled himself for what he knew he had to do. Vinnie remembered those scenes when the good guy tried to talk to the bad guy in the movies he'd seen as a kid with his uncle Andy. Uncle Andy always got angry and said, "For Christ's sake, just shoot the bastard . . . it's not worth it," and then exclaimed after the good guy got shot, "See? He'd be alright if he'd just shot'em in the first place instead of mincing words."

Vinnie told Rebecca to look away and cover her ears. She did neither. Vinnie walked into the pod without saying a word and brought his weapon up to his shoulder. He immediately recognized the leader of the Red Guard detail and the others. The same guards had beaten him when they first came to the dungeon.

"Well, look what the cat dragged in," Vinnie said vengefully.

The Red Guard leader turned, and a sinister smile came across his face when he recognized who was speaking to him.

"So, my little popinjay, you have returned to us. Perhaps we should continue where we left off; a nice little bonus, eh men?"

"I don't think so, ass-face. It's your turn for a brief lesson in humility," Vinnie said with steel in his voice.

Whatever hesitation Vinnie had held about killing someone evaporated. The smile disappeared from the leader's face, and he took on a more ominous attitude.

"We outnumber you, and I'm tired of toying with you. Seize him," the leader ordered.

Vinnie aimed, opened fire, and put three-round bursts into the men nearest him. No one drew a sword or knife. Vinnie reloaded his weapon with another thirty-round magazine and then shot the rest, who had quickly recovered from the shock, and went for their weapons.

In seconds, the men fell to the floor, dead. He went over to the leader, who had soiled himself, and butt-stroked him in the gut and head. The noise from the rifle fire became painfully deafening.

"I told you, butt breath, you've messed with the wrong people," Vinnie said to the leader before shooting him in the groin, legs, and arm.

He then took out his .45 and shot him in the forehead. Vinnie walked over to the passed-out jailer, took his keys, gave them to Rebecca, and told her to open the cell doors. She was terrified, never having experienced something so horrific in her life.

She responded to his commands like a robot as she trembled and sobbed, knowing she needed to help get everyone out of there immediately. The girls were screaming and weeping loudly. After what they'd witnessed, there was no consoling them.

In a commanding voice, Vinnie raised his hand and said, "Look, girls, please keep quiet. We don't want to draw more attention than we've already caused."

Killing these guards caused Vinnie to grow up instantly. He felt sick to his stomach, a sensation similar to seasickness. After his first kill in combat, Vinnie experienced anxiety, fear, guilt, and other complicated feelings. But he fought these feelings off.

He knew he needed to show strength to keep these kids feeling secure, especially Rebecca. Something about her was getting to him. He was falling in love. Vinnie knew that, after today, he'd never feel the same about many things again.

"Holy crap, that's gunfire!" Bailey exclaimed.

"It's right over our heads," Boz added.

"It's gotta be Vinnie . . . damn him," Doug exploded. "Now we're in really deep shit. C'mon, help me get this grate off."

The men pushed the grate aside and climbed through. To their amazement, they found themselves on the east edge of the pod of cells. Rebecca screamed when she first saw them climbing out. Vinnie whirled around, expecting more soldiers, but saw Doug instead.

Rebecca continued to calm the girls. Vinnie quickly explained to Doug what had happened and why. Doug thought about it for a moment. He knew the Red Guard had learned a lesson today, and Vinnie had gotten some revenge. He quickly concluded that everything happens for a reason based on a good one. Doug made a quick decision about what they should do next.

"Everyone, go down into the sewer," he said, pointing toward the grate. "Boz, lead the way . . . and hurry."

Doug went to Audra's open cell, where Rebecca and Vinnie stood. He saw she appeared to lie on her deathbed.

"Leave me," she croaked. "I'm not in any condition to move, and my end is near. I can feel it."

"Nonsense," Doug barked. He scooped up the old witch and carried her to the sewer grate, then hefted her over his shoulder and told her to hang on as he carried her down the ladder.

"Vinnie, you play rear guard. Rebecca, you stay with me. Let's go."

"I'm staying with Vinnie . . ."

"Rebecca! I'm not your father, but if I have to come back for you, I will spank you if you insist on acting like a spoiled brat," Doug warned her sternly.

"Whaaa . . . How dar . . ."

"Rebecca!" Vinnie said softly. "He means it. You better get your butt down there and help with Audra."

A loathsome look came across her face as she angrily marched to the sewer grate and went through it. Without exposing himself to crossbow fire, Vinnie went down a few rungs to view the corridor.

When Bailey called for him to come down, Vinnie slung the CAR-15 over his shoulder, pulled the grate cover over himself, and descended. The loud explosions echoed throughout the castle and heard by others in the dungeon complex. Many men came running to see what had happened, led by the sergeant of the guard.

When the sergeant got to the eastern pod of cells, he saw dead men lying all over the ground. A lot of blood covered the floor, but no one understood what had happened or why there weren't any drawn swords in anyone's hands.

The sergeant noticed the many small brass casings on the floor but didn't understand what they were or why there were dead soldiers. However, he quickly noticed that the cell doors were open, and the cells were empty. The women were missing . . . again.

The captain of the guard arrived and became horrified to see the carnage in front of him. He left the cleaning to the sergeant of the guard while he quickly went to report. Captain Linden went directly to the King's apartments and knocked on the door, and the guards announced him to the King.

Upon hearing of the slaughter in the dungeons and the women escaping again, the King knew his daughter had somehow involved herself in the outrage. He ordered the entire castle guard turned out to find them, including the knights and their soldiers.

"Scour the countryside." The King demanded, "until we find all the girls and they're brought back."

Inside the castle, the guards, soldiers, and horsemen formed a search party. The castle gates opened, and scores of men disbursed in all directions.

Zenega went berserk when he heard of the ladies' escape, screaming curses and threats into the darkness from the parapet of his tower. He vowed revenge and death for those responsible . . . to anyone who dared to interfere with his exorcising the ever-increasing madness from his body and mind by using his unique process of injecting his seed into the fertile egg of his consort and then feeding on the host human body of a teenaged girl.

In the distance, Zenega saw a flight of namatars heading his way. He'd diverted them to search for and destroy those who dared to get in his way . . . an act of butchery he looked forward to with relish.

Chapter XX

oz and Bailey led the girls away from the sewer, across the stream, and into the crop fields. Doug continued to carry Audra. Rebecca and Vinnie brought up the rear. Doug returned along the path he'd come from, where the tank sat hidden in the dark.

When Doug and the others regrouped at the road crossing, he pointed out the horsemen and knights riding toward them from the castle and heading in different directions. Doug led the group back across the main roadway and quickly headed west at the first chance.

The trail he took them on got little use and overgrown with weeds and grass, so it was not easily visible. Doug took the group about twenty-five yards into the crop fields before feeling they became masked enough from view. The trail there was clearer. Boz and Bailey ran ahead with the girls while Doug struggled with Audra. Vinnie stayed with them and sent Rebecca on with the rest.

"Please let me down," the witch pleaded. "I can't go on!"

"You will go on, my lady, and you will be well again. It would be best if you believed that. How else can you care for these girls?" Doug said while he hurried along.

"When you have destroyed the evil in this land, no one will need me anymore," she croaked.

"Nonsense! There is revenge to be exacted against your arch-nemesis, Zenega, and you shall have your moment . . . even if I have to carry you to him."

The old woman cackled through a painful coughing and wheezing spell.

"You are a good man, Douglas," she whispered in a voice he'd never heard her use before and in a tone reminiscent of her youth. Then she returned to her croaking pitch. "How much longer must I endure this torture?" She asked lightly.

"We're almost there," Doug lied.

Boz, Bailey, and the girls arrived at the old, abandoned hamlet in time to see namatars appear overhead without warning. They circled, looking for their prey.

One girl, Giselle, said, "I know this place! There's an old, unused wine cellar somewhere around here." She looked around in the full moonlight and pointed to the old winery shack.

"Look, over there . . . there's a large room in the cellar down the stairs. Everyone will be comfortable there," Giselle said.

"I'll keep watch for Doug and Vinnie if you want to check out the cellar," Bailey told Boz. Boz went in with his flashlight and his CAR-15, ready for action. The middle of the room had a double-wide flight of stairs; at the bottom, a set of open double doors faced him. He entered through the doors and saw an empty room filled with weeds and mushrooms. In the walls were four broken-down shelves. Boz returned to the group.

"Gather as much wood as you can, and I'll build a fire to keep you warm and toasty," Boz told the girls.

The girls responded quickly without comment; even Rebecca helped. Boz dug a fire pit with an old wooden spade he found lying on the ground and started the fire. When Doug arrived with Audra, he set her down gently on the ground near the pit.

"You girls make Audra as comfortable as possible while we take care of some business," he requested.

"We'll be right upstairs. We're not leaving you, girls, until you're all safe," Bailey assured them.

"Is that your iron war beast up there?" One girl asked.

"Yup, that's Vicky," Vinnie said proudly.

"You named your war beast?" Rebecca asked, confused.

"Of course we did. And now we need to go and whup some ass with it," Vinnie boasted.

"Huh?" Rebecca said.

"Do not leave this place, no matter what you hear coming from above, if you value your lives," Doug warned the girls.

Before Vinnie turned to leave, Rebecca grabbed his face and gave him another long, warm kiss on the lips. She said sweetly in a hushed whisper, "Please come back to me, Vinnie."

He didn't resist or say a word this time; he merely stood mesmerized, staring into her eyes. The men left and went to the fields.

The namatars continued to circle above. Then, without warning, while Doug and the crew climbed aboard Vicky, a namatar landed on the ground. It looked hideous and menacing. Vinnie, at that moment, was climbing inside the cupola. The namatar hissed and bared its needle-sharp fangs, looking like it was ready to attack. Vinnie got inside the tank, turned on the battery switch, and quickly returned to the hatch.

The men slowly aimed their CAR-15s at the creature and backed toward the hatches when it flapped its wings and lurched back, preparing to leap at them. Then the creature bounded forward, and Vinnie turned the cupola and opened fire with the .50, suspending the creature in mid-flight as red tracer bullets ripped through its ugly torso, cutting it into shreds.

As it hit the ground, the namatar emitted an ear-piercing death cry similar to fingernails scratching a blackboard. The dying cry reverberated through everyone's nervous system. The men quickly climbed inside the tank, took their stations, and put their helmets on. Vinnie jumped into the driver's seat and cranked Vicky over, and the tank came to full power.

"Pull her out and back up a bit to keep the wine cellar covered," Doug advised.

Two more namatars flew over the tank and turned for another pass. Bailey opened fire on them with his M60 machine gun without Doug telling him to do so. The machine gun, already locked into its mount near the loader's hatch, gave Bailey easy access to them. He walked the tracers directly into the namatars.

They both dropped from the sky like bricks. The crew heard another bloodcurdling scream that sounded like a wounded animal killed by a predator or a furious beast in the distance. They even saw a flash of bright light in the eastern sky. The sight of the two namatars being knocked out of the air by a trail of red dots had not gone unnoticed.

The noise and the sight of tracers going into the night sky caught the attention of the castle horsemen, guards, and knights. They had reformed at the front of the castle and intended to ride through the cornfield toward the source of the strange activity.

Doug called out, following standard operating procedure, "Gunner, enemy personnel, twelve o'clock, canister, load."

The genuine test of their months of training to defend themselves was now at hand.

Bailey removed a canister tank round from the ammunition storage rack and loaded it into the 105-millimeter main tank gun.

"Canister up!" Bailey responded, slamming the round into the breach.

"Fire!" Doug yelled.

They obliterated the first mass of horsemen that came galloping toward them in one instant by unleashing thousands of miniature ball bearings from the tank's main gun. The projectiles spread out like those in a shotgun blast, leaving nothing standing in their wake. Horses, men, uniforms, leather, and iron plates all disintegrated in the path of fire. More namatars swooped in, flying over the tank.

"Bailey, Boz, load the canister on your own, choose your targets frugally, and fire. I'm going to be busy shooting namatars with the fifty. Vinnie, come up into Bailey's hatch and use the M60 on them," Doug commanded.

Vinnie quickly climbed into Bailey's hatch to control the machine gun better, making it easier to shoot from inside the turret. Each time Boz fired a canister round, it rocked the tank and threw Vinnie's aim off.

Doug and Vinnie destroyed four more namatars. The King's men retreated to the castle. Boz and Bailey had delivered the horsemen a devastating blow from which they would never recover. The captain of the guard never knew the escaped prisoners were the ones responsible for their defeat.

The senior knight, the captains of the household cavalry, and the guards all ran to the King. He'd taken a position atop the castle balcony over the front gates. Together, they told him about the horror in the crop fields west of the castle.

"Your Majesty!" The captain of the household cavalry said, visibly shaken. "An unknown enemy has attacked us and savaged our forces. We have lost many men to a weapon so gruesome that we cannot explain it," the senior knight said.

"Yes, it even destroyed many namatars, fellingthem from the sky," the captain of the guard added.

Confused and frightened, the King asked, "I was watching from here when the noise began. Where are your men now?"

"Those of us left have all returned to the castle for safety, Your Majesty," the captain of the cavalry said.

"The men are protecting the ramparts and have taken fighting positions to repel any attack on the castle," the senior knight added.

"This will displease Lord Zenega, I fear," the King said with concern.

"Your Majesty," General Gaiet said, rushing to the King's side.

"I just heard the news. What are your orders?" He asked, out of breath.

The King merely stared into the darkness beyond the castle. A squeaking and clanking noise emanated from off in the distance. It was a strange noise the King and his staff had never heard before in the Kingdom. In the darkness, a hulking behemoth neared, its long snout moving left and right like a tentacle.

"Everyone to their stations," Doug bellowed. "Vinnie, make a left turn and head for the road to the castle. Let's turn on the Tank Thermal Sights (TTS), the gun stabilizer, and the Infrared (IR). Boz, you keep a search going for any enemy targets."

"Okay, sarge, but what about the girls?"

"I think it's better if we stay away from them for now so we don't draw unwanted attention to this old hamlet. I don't want to give anyone any ideas," Doug said.

"Sarge, I got the road, and I can see the castle lit up. I'm turning right," Vinnie announced.

"Good. Boz, let me know the second you spot something. I need to stay on the fifty. You use the co-ax if you have to," Doug ordered.

The co-ax was the M240, a 7.62 mm co-axial machine gun mounted parallel to the main tank gun.

"Vinnie, bring the tank to a stop about two hundred meters before getting to the water fountain. I want to be close and personal when we rip this place down to its underwear."

"You got it, sarge," Vinnie replied.

Zenega's madness went from bad to worse, to unmanageable. He teetered on the verge of losing total control over his human form. Even

Melonjack didn't know who or what his master was, and neither did anyone else in the Kingdom.

Zenega had watched the chain of events occur from the western window of his tower when he heard of the massacre of his men in the dungeon. He roiled at the destruction of his beloved namatars. He received telepathic waves from his consort, who agonized over their deaths. For the namatars, in actuality, were their children.

Zenega heard her cry and feared she'd soon rise and destroy this culture. If the bloodbath continued and she didn't stop this intruder, he would have to do it soon. The King's men, nothing more than an inept bunch of sissies, put the onus on Zenega to assemble his Red Guard and send them to find and destroy this enemy to the peace. His Red Guard, his invincibles, would go forth to save the day.

"Sarge, I got multiple targets between twelve and two o'clock," Boz said.

"What are they, infantry?" Doug asked.

"Looks like it."

"Okay, everyone, get on a machine gun," ordered Doug.

The crew took their positions. Doug saw men dressed in red advancing toward them with their swords drawn and shields up. When the men got within three hundred meters, Doug heard them banging on their shields with their swords, an ancient ploy to scare the waiting foe.

"Open fire!" Doug ordered.

Three machine guns lashed their red tongues of death, but the men continued advancing.

"Ceasefire," Doug ordered.

"Okay, I guess we have a problem," Doug said. "Gunner! Target, infantry, load HE."

Bailey again selected the appropriate antipersonnel ammunition and loaded it into the main gun.

"HE up!" Bailey called.

"Fire!"

The main gun of the M60A3 tank recoiled as it sent the round of M393 twenty-five-pound high explosive (RDX) round hurtling toward the Red Guard at 2,241 feet per second. The first round landed right in the closest formation, instantly blowing ten men into pieces.

The second and third rounds reduced the formation by twenty more soldiers. The men watched the last twenty soldiers drop their swords and shields and run for cover in the castle. As they did so, Doug and the crew shot them all in their backs with machine guns. Without the protection of their shields, they fell like the cowards they were. Only five survived to tell the tale to Zenega.

The King and his staff watched the dreaded and feared Red Guard get decimated right in front of their eyes from the balcony. To the King, nothing seemed able to stop whatever this monster was, and nothing explained either why or what the thing wanted.

"Your Majesty, I think it would be wise if I took a white flag and attempted to contact this beast, to speak with it and see what it wishes of us," General Gaiet advised the King.

The King gave the general his permission to do this. General Gaiet got a horse and a white flag and rode slowly toward the tank.

"Sarge, we've got a visitor," Vinnie said.

Doug opened his hatch and stood on his seat. He saw a rider approaching with a white flag.

"I'm going out to meet with him; keep me covered. Vinnie, take the fifty cal.," Doug ordered.

Doug climbed out of his hatch and dropped from the tank. He walked about ten yards from the tank toward the approaching figure. The general dismounted and walked to Doug.

"You're human," the general said, surprised.

"What'd you expect, men from Mars?" Doug asked, pointing toward the stars.

"Ah ... no, of course not ... I didn't know what to expect," confided the general.

"I'm Platoon Sergeant Douglas Baker, C Company, Third Platoon, One Forty-third Armor."

The general did not understand what the man he faced said, so he introduced himself.

"I am General Gaiet, commander of the King's guards and cavalry. I'm here to ask your intentions. . . and what this . . . this . . . thing is."

"General, I don't suppose you have the slightest idea of the tremendous power that faces you. You're also unaware that we are the escaped prisoners everyone has been looking for."

His mouth went agape. "No, I was not aware," he said, surprised. "I had not seen you before; therefore, I would have never known. Now I understand. You want revenge."

"No, general. We want to stop Zenega and the atrocities he perpetrates on these young girls in your kingdom."

"So, it is true; you came to disturb our peace."

"No, general, we didn't. But that's what ended up happening," Doug said resolutely.

Doug attempted to explain the events of how they had mysteriously arrived in this kingdom. It seemed challenging to elucidate modern physics to an eighteenth-century mind, much less the presence of a fifty-two-ton M60A3 tank.

"Rebecca, help me up. I have to see what is happening," Audra pleaded.

"The men said we must stay here, my lady," Rebecca said.

"Only you and I will go; the rest of the girls must stay, that is true. I Have to be near Vicky, the iron war beast; she calls me," Audra explained.

"How is it that an iron war beast can call you? It's made of iron," Rebecca asked naively.

Audra cocked her head to one side and gave the princess a questioning, impatient look. Rebecca took the cue and helped the old woman to her feeble feet. She handed Audra her walking stick, and they shuffled up the stairs and into the crop field, following the trail of Vicky's tracks.

They heard the fire of the machine guns and saw the tracers and muzzle flashes from the tank. It developed into a frightening sight. They sought a safe place to the south of Vicky.

The women found a cutout in the crop field where a small grape storage bin had once stood and an old, elevated, stone stomping pit. They took shelter within the pit, which masked them from anyone who might try to see them from high atop the castle walls.

The two women sat and watched the battle until the general rode up to speak with Doug. They were near enough to hear what the two men spoke about.

"Your tale is very confusing," the general said to Doug with dedication. "I must accept that there is a semblance of truth to what you say because of the presence of this iron monster, but I am honor-bound to protect and defend my king and his kingdom to the death."

"General, we are not here to fight your king, feebleminded as he may be, to allow such atrocities to occur within his kingdom. Our goal is to stop what is happening here. We can do whatever it takes, including the destruction of your castle. We will take out all the men within it and do whatever else we have to do to defeat your sorcerer," Doug said with resolve. "Have you or the King any idea what that fiend does with the young girls?"

"No, I don't; no one does. I am forbidden to ask," the general replied.

"Well, let me clarify what your sorcerer is up to." Doug explained, "I understand the King is under Zenega's spell, and that is why this brutality is allowed to go on." The blood drained from the general's face as Doug revealed the secret. He exhibited a sick appearance, thinking about the words he'd heard.

"You see, general, you've been complicit in this atrocity."

"I . . . I don't know what to say," the general stammered, trying to speak.

"Then go back and tell your king what you know. My ultimatum is simple. Either destroy Zenega, or I will destroy your king, your castle, and Zenega."

Doug returned to Vicky as a giant ball of fire came from inside the castle and landed just short of its intended target. General Gaiet had mounted his horse and headed back toward the castle, wondering what devil would launch fireballs at him while under a flag of truce.

"Hey, sarge, they must have one of those catapults," Vinnie said as he climbed back into the driver's seat of the tank when Doug dropped in through his commander's hatch. Abruptly, more fireballs arced from inside the castle and landed around Vickie, setting the dry crops ablaze.

"They're going to burn us out!" Bailey said.

"Boz, start putting some rounds into the castle walls and front door; I can see many of them on the ramparts," Doug said. "But watch your ammo. We still have a lot of fighting to do."

Boz and Bailey fired three rounds from the main gun into the castle's front wall, reducing the façade to rubble. Then, after Boz loaded the fourth round, Vicky moved her turret, aimed her gun right at Zenega's tower complex, and fired. The entire top floor disappeared in a cloud of fire and smoke.

"Holy crap, did you see that?" Vinnie exclaimed.

"I didn't tell you to shoot that tower," Doug said to Boz, surprised.

"I didn't," Boz replied. "Vicky did it herself."

Audra cackled with glee as she lowered her walking stick. "See, child? There's still some magic left in this old stick. It was my mother's, you know."

Rebecca looked on, dumbstruck. "That was Zenega's tower," she said in a hushed tone.

"Yes, it was . . . but I doubt I hurt him. Though perhaps I made him soil himself." She cackled with joy.

"But, my lady, he will be furious," Rebecca said, concerned.

"Fear not yet, child. There is still a long night ahead of us. The consort will rise at the stroke of midnight," Audra warned.

"What? Whose consort? Oh my, the she-devil!" Rebecca said as she realized about who the witch was referring to.

"Bailey, what time is it?" Doug asked. His face was in his commander's eyepiece, working the laser range finder.

"Just about midnight," he responded.

´Chapter XXI

The stroke of midnight rang its last note from the giant clock tower, signaling the conclusion of another day and the beginning of a new one. Zenega was slowly recovering from the destruction of his residence.

The uppermost part of the tower looked like hand-pulverized stone. Zenega lay in a pile of debris on the floor below what had once been his dwelling. His trusty apprentice lay dead next to him. Getting to his feet didn't trouble him. He knew no harm could come to him because of the nonhuman bonding of his skin's cell structure. Many years before he had come here, he'd experimented, searching for a potion to give longevity to human organs.

He had collected the remains of dead dragons and used their body parts in much of his work.

Instead, he accidentally discovered a formula that gave him the ability to have the toughness of a dragon's skin and resistance to fire. The last potion he developed gave him only the tough skin and not the longevity he sought. An unexpected side effect of this potion gave him the ability to transform himself into the flying terror everyone feared.

This transformation only happens when induced under the spell of madness. Zenega did not always have complete control, which resulted from his experiments. And he wasn't alone in this ability.

He looked into the moonlit night and thought of his one true love. Zenega knew the last day of October was upon them. He envisioned the hate and anger probably overwhelming her. She'll rise, take to the sky, and avenge her dead. She'll destroy those responsible and those who failed the pledge to keep the peace.

The moon rose, and out of her lair, she came, the cave within the mountain trembling beneath her heavy feet. She'd not found one host to plant her eggs in, and she moved in a rage she'd never felt before, exacerbated by the death of some of her children. This will be the day. If there is not a host provided to me, she swore to incinerate everything and everyone in the Kingdom.

She marched from the mouth of the small canyon to the edge of a ridge and took flight. Her long, broad wingspan carried her into the moon-filled night. She wanted and severely needed to destroy something. Vicky's turret turned right and elevated by itself. Boz immediately looked into the main gun sight.

"Sarge! We've got company, and you will not believe what it is," Boz yelled.

Doug and the crew went through the hatches and stood on top of the turret. The outline of a dragon appeared across the moon. The moonlight radiated off her skin as she flew back and forth across the sky. Flying toward her went the remaining namatars. They circled and searched not only for the girls, but also for Vicky.

"Christ, look at the size of that thing!" Vinnie proclaimed. "What d'ya think about the size of a semi? Bailey asked Boz.

"Yeah, head to tail and a few thousand pounds," Boz replied.

"She looks dark gray, and I bet she can belch a fiery flame," Bailey said.

"Button uuuup!" Yelled Doug. "Get ready for a big fight."

"Geez, which round do you want to use on that thing?" Bailey asked as he and the rest of the crew raced back inside Vicky.

"Try the HEAT-T," Doug suggested. "Boz, you'll have to wait until that thing sits down somewhere. You're not shooting a multi-fire anti-aircraft gun, you know!"

"Yeah, I know. It's going to be dicey at best," Boz replied.

Doug watched the dragon fly toward the castle. First, she focused on spitting fire. Then she picked up large pieces of rubble and heaved them at the occupants with her short, stubby, yet powerful arms. Men, all ablaze, fell or jumped from the ramparts.

"If that bitch hovers for just a second, I'm gonna blast her," Boz said.

No further comment was necessary. Boz struggled to keep a bead on the dragon. She swooped in and out of proximity to the tank. Since the aerial attack concentrated on the castle, Doug told Vinnie to get on the M60 up top again while he worked the .50.

"Use anything except ball ammo on those things," Doug advised everyone. "Let's try to take out some more of those namatars."

Doug and the crew changed the ammunition in their machine guns to armor-piercing or incendiary. They aimed at the namatars and opened fire. Again, Vicky lit up like a Roman candle and spewed tracers. More namatars fell dead and wounded. The dragon came to a complete stop in mid-flight and hovered there for a second, her eyes ablaze, turning to identify from where the attack on her children had originated.

That moment of hesitation was all Boz needed. He focused the laser dot right on the dragon's belly, locked the thermal sighting reticle on the target, hit the Ammunition Select Unit switch, got a ballistic solution from the computer, gripped the gunner's handles, and, with his thumbs, pressed the firing buttons.

Vicky lurched back as she spit twenty-three pounds of an M456 series High-Explosive Antitank round with a tracer. They watched the red phosphor trail go from Vicky straight into the dragon. The force of the blow knocked the dragon backward out of the sky. She went into the castle and destroyed every structure in her wake.

She came to rest somewhere in the medieval compound behind the castle. Doug and the men then finished destroying the rest of the namatars. There was no time for raucous celebrations, though. They thought they'd killed the dragon but had only further infuriated an already irate beast.

The dragon flew out of the ruins, her enormous talons clawing for altitude. She focused on the location where her prey sat. She turned toward her target, swooped in, flared, reared back with her wings extended, and drenched the tank with her breath of fire.

Buttoned up and expecting a retaliatory attack, Doug waited for another clear shot at her. He saw that the antitank round had hit her and caused surface damage, but it had not penetrated her scaly skin. Her fire, hot enough to kill a human and burn wooden structures, could not harm fifty-two tons of steel.

After she flew off, Doug and the crew got busy trying to locate her again, but couldn't. Then Vicky turned her turret and pointed the main gun right at the dragon, hiding off to the right side of the castle, examining her wounds. Vicky laid the laser range finder on the dragon and set the shot up again.

Bailey loaded another M393 HEP-T round. Vicky fired it, and then he reloaded again. The round caught the dragon by surprise, striking her in the neck while her head had turned, and she licked her wounds. The explosion knocked her off her haunches and into the irrigation ditch.

"Boy, I bet that pissed her off," Boz said, chuckling.

Again, the dragon came off the ground, angrier than before, and zoomed right in on Vicky. The beast landed on the tank, clawed and bit, and snapped at it. The men couldn't seem to get a gun on her. Vinnie drove erratically through the crop fields, causing the thing to lose its balance and fall off the tank.

Her wings flapped determinedly to stay on the tank, but the slick steel offered no stable footing. Doug watched the dragon through the view ports of the cupola. When he saw her clamping her jaws around the big radio antenna, he reached down and turned the selector switch from intercom to FM transmit and squeezed his mic button.

Instantly, over fifty thousand volts of static electricity burst through the antenna. The shock knocked the dragon off the tank with a heavy thud, putting her in a daze. Immediately, Vinnie turned around and headed back toward the dragon at full speed. During the excitement, Bailey inadvertently loaded a hypervelocity, armor-piercing, discarding sabot round, an M735 HVAP-DS-T.

The dragon got to her feet again. This time, she didn't have the agility that she'd had before. She needed to run on her stubby legs before trying to take flight. She stumbled twice, got to her feet, and made an attempt. The dragon needed to take a break before fighting her assailant again, but the crew didn't feel merciful.

Vicky kept on her trail and chased her all over the fields, firing her machine guns. Finally, the dragon took flight and distanced herself from the tank. Doug peppered her wings with .50-caliber fire. She flew around, regaining her strength and altitude before zeroing in on her foe again. The crew brought Vicky back to a position five hundred meters from the castle.

"I think this is where we separate the chaff from the wheat, men," Doug said. "I think that jolt did a lot of damage to that thing."

The dragon returned for another attack. The moon disappeared behind a cloud and denied the crew a silhouette of the beast. She flew in from the northeast using a spread-winged position, preparing to blow fire on Vicky again.

She flared and hovered in front of Vicky and filled her lungs, but before she got one puff out, Boz fired on her. The round sent thirteen pounds of tungsten carbide right through her chest. It exited on the right side of her spine through her shoulder blade. The dragon felt the round sever her arteries, pierce her heart, cause massive internal bleeding, and blow out her back.

She could feel the force of the round strike her and push her back about one hundred yards, causing her to expel fiery breath from her lungs, which helped propel her back even further through the air.

Doug and the crew watched her drop like a rock into the large pond northeast of the castle. She was dead before she hit bottom. Doug credited the jolt of electricity with changing the dynamics of her cell structure and removing her skin's protection, allowing the round to penetrate.

Doug told the men to open the tank's hatches to let in some cool night air. He climbed out and sat on the turret to catch his breath. The crew rejoiced over their impressive but fleeting victory. Doug reminded them there was still another menace they must contend with . . . the male.

Doug expected him to come to do battle and seek revenge. He expected the male to have more power and strength and would not be as easy to defeat as the female. Doug heard some rustling in the flattened crops to their south. Two figures slowly emerged from the darkness, walking toward them. Doug recognized Audra struggling on her cane, with Rebecca assisting her.

"What the devil are you two doing out here? Don't you know you could get killed or injured?" Doug said worriedly from his seat in the cupola.

"My lady wishes to speak with you," Rebecca said. Doug quickly climbed off the tank.

"We have been watching you from the start," Audra said weakly. Doug went pale. "The last battle is with Zenega himself. He has become like his consort. The potions he experimented with years ago have turned him into the hideous monster you will witness shortly. The female, it is said, was at one time a beautiful woman before Zenega's experiments."

"You mean that dragon we just killed was a real woman once?" Doug asked in disbelief.

"Yes, and the namatars were her flawed and deformed children. Zenega consumes himself with the acquisition of power. He will stop at nothing to gain it and destroy anyone or anything that gets in his way. He was building an army of namatars to help him in his conquests," Audra explained.

"I'm sure he will be along any minute to exact his revenge. You both need to get to shelter," Doug said firmly.

"No, not just yet. Zenega has a flaw. In the center of his chest is a deformity. You must strike him there twice, in that exact spot. The first will open the deformity; the second will destroy him," Audra persisted. "Your strikes must occur one after the other; otherwise, they will not be sufficient to . . ."

She went into a coughing and wheezing spell again. Rebecca took her, and they turned to go back to the grape-stomping pit.

Doug looked at the other men and said, "You heard the lady; we need a one-two punch to take him out."

The women returned to their hiding place, and the crew prepared to do more battle.

´Chapter XXII

Zenega stood on a rampart and watched. Overcome with horror and anger. He saw his consort and their children attempt to exact revenge on the castle dwellers, and this iron menace who'd arrived on this land to ruin everything he had plotted for and built.

The castle had become reduced to rubble, nearly destroyed. Many men and women had died, victims of their self-indulgence and avarice. The rest of the population tried to extinguish the fires caused by the fighting.

Zenega, under great torment, had finally reached his point of no return. As the potions within his body overwhelmed his physiological stability and anger fueled him, he passed a threshold from beyond which his body refused to return.

Zenega transformed himself from a human into a flying aberration, like his consort, through a long and painful process whereby mortal flesh becomes immortal wyvern, only bigger and more powerful.

"Sarge, I got a bad feeling," Vinnie said, looking toward the castle and watching the glowing fires. "We haven't seen that dude Zenega, and I think he's weird, and something's gonna happen. I can feel it."

"Perhaps you're right, Vinnie. We need to keep our eyes open and be even more vigilant," Doug suggested.

"What the hell did you load that last time, Bailey?" Boz asked.

"It was a HVAPDS (Antitank Round) round. I loaded it by mistake," Bailey replied, reading the information from the spent shell casing.

"Good mistake, I'd say," Vinnie chimed.

Vicky's turret whirred and turned toward the ruins of Zenega's old tower. Her gun elevated.

"Okay, guys, that's our signal; it's time to go to war again," Doug alerted the men.

Doug and the crew quickly climbed aboard Vicky, donned their helmets, and took their stations. Doug knew this last battle would determine his and everyone else's fate. This fight intended to defend good over evil.

He looked through his periscope and sights, trying to spot the threat. Something hit the tank on the left side from nowhere, raising it off its track a few feet.

"Vinnie, get this thing moving and keep it moving. Do zigzags or something," Doug bellowed.

Vinnie stomped on the accelerator pedal and propelled Vicky away from whatever had struck them; they suspected it was Zenega. The men tried frantically to locate the threat. Vinnie drove erratically, which didn't help and instead complicated matters, even if it was a necessary maneuver.

Vinnie, led by frustration, opened his hatch so he could see better. He glimpsed something flying toward him from the left, steered the tank with the T-bar, and caused the gun to get directly aimed at the flying aberration.

Vinnie screamed into his intercom, "Target twelve o'clock and closing!"

Doug found himself in an unconventional combat condition, which he was quickly adapting to. Rediscovering his courage and determination, he fought the best way he could. He knew he couldn't apply his training and experience because its intended use against other armored vehicles did not fit the profile.

The shooting procedure called for identifying a target, selecting the best ammunition to defeat it, and the order to fire. But now, the rule book was out, and total initiative and adaptability was in. Bailey expected what he thought was the best ammunition to use. He loaded an armor-piercing round and pre-chambered it so it would fire when Boz needed it.

Boz positioned the turret, laying the laser rangefinder on the incoming specter. He turned on the main gun stabilization switch, set the shot up, firmly gripped the trigger handle, and was about to shoot when Doug opened fire with the .50.

He laid a stream of armor-piercing incendiary tracers right into Zenega's left wing and caused the behemoth to swerve up and to the left. Boz locked onto him with the main gun. Zenega exposed his belly then, and Boz pressed the firing button.

The tank round rocketed out of the rifled bore. It exploded right between Zenega's legs, knocking his back end and tail section into the air and turning his head nose-down. Zenega lost control of himself. He spiraled to his left, went vertical, and hit the ground on his head, followed by the rest of his body with a thunderous thud. Doug couldn't believe his eyes. Zenega had transformed into a dragon. His body was a royal blue and longer and heavier than the females. He had a row of dorsal fins down his back and long, spiny protrusions extending from the sides of his neck like withers.

Vinnie, hearing Zenega land with a thud and a grunt, quickly closed his hatch in expectation of the fiery blast . . . but it didn't come. Instead, Zenega got to his feet, lowered his head, and charged toward the tank like an elephant. Boz fired the HE round Bailey had loaded, and Doug ordered the crew to open fire with machine guns.

Doug fired a volley of smoke grenades from the smoke dispensers on the front of the turret. Vinnie cut a hard right and headed toward the castle, where the fires gave out more light.

Zenega flew off to the north, cut east, and descended to treetop level. Doug anticipated this and told Vinnie to drive back to the concealment of the smoke cloud. When they arrived, Vinnie found a large, shady tree and hid the tank behind it. As he approached from the southeast, Zenega got a surprise.

He couldn't see the tank anywhere. He hovered for a minute and then got nailed again by a HEAT round, hitting him under the right wing pit; the exploding metal tore a minor but irritating gash along his rib cage. Zenega rolled to the left, flew south, gained altitude, turned right, and swooped in.

He landed on top of Vicky, clawing and scratching at her. His talons squashed the M60 machine gun Bailey had used. He twisted off the barrel of the Browning M2 .50-caliber machine gun with his hands. He then leaned over the front of the tank and attempted to bend the main gun with his stubby arms. Vicky bent her FM antenna, so it touched Zenega's tail. Again, she engaged the FM radio, sending an enormous jolt of static electricity all over the tank, frying Zenega's scaly skin.

Much to Doug's chagrin, this last shock burned out the radio, short-circuited the electrical system, and put the interior of the tank into total darkness. Vinnie drove evasively again. He twisted and turned Vicky's massive frame, finally hurling the hulking dragon to the ground.

"Vinnie, slow down a minute and turn back toward the target. Boz, reset the circuit breaker on the TTS," Doug yelled.

He opened his hatch after Zenega fell off, grabbed a spare .50-caliber barrel from a receptacle inside his commander's module, and replaced the twisted one. Doug knew his crew's training for working in adverse conditions was adequate, but not in conditions as damaging as these. He ordered the crew to check their battle stations.

Bailey grabbed the first round he could find and rammed it into the breech. Doug hand-cranked the turret to face Zenega, but he'd flown away. He was probably planning on coming to their blind spot for another attack.

Zenega rammed Vicky broadside again with all his might to knock the tank onto its side, but he failed. He missed the center of her mass and succeeded only in spinning her around and rattling the crew. Vinnie knew the two entities did not weigh the same, but a fifty-two-ton tank was denser than a flesh-and-blood dragon. He regained his composure and drove evasively again to keep Zenega off balance.

"Vinnie, drive over to the south edge of the castle; we need our backs against something so we can stand and fight," Doug ordered.

He set up his fighting position at the southeast corner of the castle so they had a 270-degree field of vision around them. If Zenega wanted to fight, he must attack from a less-than-opportune direction.

Doug told the men to open their hatches and look around. Bailey saw Zenega diving again, this time from the north, and called out the direction. Doug and Boz manually aimed the gun tube at Zenega in a hurry.

Bailey and Vinnie frantically tried to restore electrical power by locating and recycling circuit breakers, but nothing worked. Vinnie knew Vicky's engine continued to run because it worked on compression rather than electrical ignition.

Zenega swooped in. Boz elected not to fire. Doug assumed the dragon was testing its foe to determine if it continued to have any fight left in it. He flew to the south, did a chandelle, and returned to the castle, where he landed near the demolished front doors and wall. He picked up huge chunks of debris and threw them at the tank with the same velocity as a rifle.

Doug again called the crew to button up. The chunks of debris would rarely hurt a tank, but Zenega had laced them with some energy. Doug noticed the blows were packing much more power than normal debris; he hoped they weren't too much for Vicky to withstand. The rocks flew through the air at a terrific speed, sporting blazing tails and resembling comets. Each strike rocked the tank and shook the crew to where they couldn't maintain their balance.

"Vinnie, get us outta here," screamed Doug, manually turning the cupola toward Zenega.

Vinnie pulled Vicky away from the wall and turned the tank 270 degrees, using the castle's south wall for cover from the incessant pounding Zenega inflicted. Doug continued to operate in darkness. Zenega ran out of things to throw at the tank and took off to the north, looking for a better position to use his breath of fire on the tank.

He circled behind the castle's left to come in behind his adversaries. When Zenega turned in to attack, much to his surprise, Vicky wasn't there. Bewildered, he came to a stop in midair. Hovering, he moved his massive head left and right, searching for his adversary.

Before Zenega could respond, another HEP-T round slammed him upside his neck. It crashed him into the south wall, demolishing a portion. This time, the hit left a bruise. Earlier, Vinnie had backed Vicky down the embankment and behind a copse of trees to the right, beyond the stream, masking her from Zenega's view.

Boz and Bailey set up the shot with the manual sights, knowing that when Zenega came around the corner, he must hover to send fire from his mouth, at which point Boz would shoot him. "Vinnie, get us up to the castle and down the road to that old tree again," Doug ordered.

Vinnie stomped on the accelerator pedal, drove up the embankment, turned left, and headed toward the road. Zenega came off the castle wall and clawed for altitude, his anger and frustration growing ever more intense. He'd find the men and use his fire against them.

He knew his fire burned hotter and penetrated deeper than his consorts.

However, using it took away much of his strength and made him momentarily vulnerable. He saw the tank racing along the road from a distance, heading west. He swooped in from behind them, flared his wings, drew back his head, and unleashed a flame that stretched over a hundred meters.

It caught Vicky right in the exhaust grates. Vinnie couldn't see the engine and transmission temperature gauges going into the red arc, but everyone felt it. The tank's interior heated to a point where it was nearly impossible to touch anything inside it without being burned.

From his cupola, Doug saw the outside of the tank radiating a bright orange glow. Heat and smoke billowed off the steel. Vinnie put Vicky into a hard right turn, breaking away from Zenega's stream of fire. The engine lost power and sputtered.

He knew Zenega eventually needed to take a breath. Vinnie raced toward the pond and drove right in. The orange glow diminished. Steam formed everywhere, engulfing the tank. Zenega went around for another pass and shot another stream of fire at the tank, slowly regaining his strength. Doug watched the steam rise around the overheated surfaces of the tank, temporarily masking it from view.

Bailey grabbed another round in the dark while the others opened the hatches for cool air. Vinnie drove deeper into the water to cool Vicky off fast. Doug figured that Zenega likely planned to come around and attack from the south again, so he ordered Vinnie to turn the tank south and drive it out of the pond.

He didn't want to mire the tank down in the muck. The engine quit when Vinnie downshifted into a lower gear to keep power going to the tracks. Complete silence engulfed the inside and outside of the tank. The moon set in the west. Zenega came at them again, this time from the south, as they had predicted.

Vinnie tried to restart the tank. Vicky's engine sputtered and died again from the overheating, which had caused her crankcase oil to boil. Boz and Doug manually cranked the turret toward the direction Zenega was approaching. Vinnie tried desperately to restart Vicky's big Continental V12 engine, with little success. Doug knew the fuel tank would explode with one more blast from Zenega, blowing them into oblivion.

Zenega bore down for what he knew was the final kill. He flared his wings again, extending them. It allowed him to come to and maintain his position in the air about a hundred meters from the tank. He reared his head back, took a deep breath, and blew out with all his might. The blast of fire roared across the pond and engulfed the tank.

To Doug's amazement, the pond miraculously absorbed most of the heat and protected the tank and the crew. Steam filled the air again and rose to the sky like a fog. Boz pulled the manual firing handle and sent another round into Zenega's throat, throwing off his aim. Bailey quickly reloaded.

Audra and Rebecca saw the disabled tank sitting in the pond. Vicky no longer had any strength, and Audra felt the beast's passion quickly dying. She told Rebecca to help her to her feet. Then Audra aimed her cane at Vicky, closed her eyes, and whispered something in a strange language before collapsing from exhaustion.

At that moment, Vicky's engine kicked over, and the lights and fire control systems returned online. Vinnie jammed the accelerator pedal down, drove forward, and eased Vicky to the right, trying not to get stuck in the muck. Somewhat cooler, the tank reached dry land, still under cover of the fog.

Doug told Vinnie to head back to their position near the water fountain. The men again opened the hatches for air. Zenega couldn't see through the fog and flew off. When he came around, he saw the tank on the road near the castle and zoomed in.

"Sarge! He's inbound again," Vinnie yelled.

"Button up!"

Doug jumped into his cupola; Boz's fingers flew over his range finder and stabilization switches, reset the fire control computer, and locked the targeting system on Zenega. Vinnie drove erratically to keep Zenega's aim off. The main gun followed Zenega's movements like a mongoose on a cobra.

The dragon flared again, hovered, reared his head, and came forward again, blowing its fiercest blast. Boz pressed the firing buttons with Doug working the .50 caliber. Unbeknownst to him, Bailey had loaded an APFSDS-T M735 round, which sent a 12.8-pound depleted uranium round at Zenega.

On her own, Vicky adjusted her gun tube just enough so the round would strike Zenega in the soft spot in his chest. After Boz fired, Bailey reached over for another round. To his astonishment, Vicky selected the correct round for him by highlighting it with a soft glow.

Bailey grabbed the round and slammed it into the breech. Vicky came to an abrupt stop. The sabot hit Zenega directly on the soft spot on his chest and caused his fiery blast to come to a choking halt in his throat, making him gasp.

Bailey yelled, "Up!" to Boz, who fired again.

This time, an M416 white phosphorus round left Vicky's stinger, raced up into the now-larger hole in the dragon's chest, struck a bone, and exploded. Zenega felt the burning-hot, white phosphorus explode in every direction within his body, rupturing organs, muscles, and sinews.

It penetrated his lungs, full of the flammable gas excreted by his glands, and ignited them. Doug watched in wonder as the night sky filled with the entertainment of an enormous fireball and fireworks display ever seen at Castle Darpon.

Bright light instantly radiated in every direction, accented by various colors. First, the ball projected outward. Then it fell from the sky, dimmed, and showered everything within two hundred meters with blood, guts, and other body parts, many of which landed on the tank.

Doug told the crew to open the hatches and stick their heads out a moment later. The foulest stench ever imagined greeted them, not knowing what to expect. The tank, covered with burning, smoldering flesh, crept forward. Vinnie drove toward where they had last seen Rebecca and Audra.

Zenega's head and tail, or what became left of them, landed in two places and lay burning in the crop fields. A figure ran out of the shadows when Vinnie turned Vicky to the right. Vinnie came to an immediate halt.

"Vinnie, come quick, it's Audra! I think she's dying," Rebecca cried, standing before his driver's hatch.

Doug and the men carefully dismounted the tank. The surface was now very slippery with blood and other bodily fluids. Rebecca led them to the grape-stomping pit, where Audra lay on her back. Dawn softly rose to the east, the sky cloudless and the last of the stars fading. Doug and the crew kneeled by the dying witch.

"Audra," Doug called, taking her hand in his, "what can I do for you?"

She opened her eyes and softly said, "Nothing more, my prince; my time has come, and I must depart this world for a better place. You have saved my life and fulfilled your duty." She closed her eyes and let out her last breath.

Doug folded her hands across her chest and stood up. The rest of the crew bowed their heads. Doug gathered the group to discuss the arrangements for Audra's burial. Suddenly, a vortex of white light emanated from Audra's midsection.

The men jumped back; Vinnie grabbed Rebecca and held her close to him, protecting her from any dangers caused by this phenomenon. The vortex grew broader and higher, spinning faster and faster, engulfing Audra's whole body.

The light was so bright that Doug shielded his eyes and looked away. As abruptly as the light had arrived, it disappeared. Lying in the place of the old, deformed witch, Doug saw a tall, slender woman of radiant beauty with long black hair and a long, purple-laced robe. Doug could not believe his eyes. The spell had broken and Audra returned to her former self. Rebecca rushed to her side and took her hand.

"Audra . . . Audra," she called.

Audra slowly opened her eyes and smiled. "Would someone please help me up?" She asked groggily, taking a deep breath. The crew reached for and grabbed Audra's hands and arms and hoisted her to her feet.

"What the hell just happened?" Doug asked, bewildered.

"When you destroyed Zenega, everything he had done reverted to its original status. Along with him, everything he couldn't restore got destroyed. . . the spells and curses. Now we can live in peace and safety," she said, "and a maniacal madman will no longer subject young girls to his whims."

The sun emerged on the horizon. A beautiful day awaited. Five riders from the castle approached the place where everyone stood. Doug immediately drew his sidearm, but Audra put her hand gently on Doug's right forearm, signifying there was no longer any danger from these men. Doug relaxed the grip on his pistol.

The captain of the guard, Captain Bedwell, asked, "Princess, are you all right?" He dismounted and walked to the group.

He looked at Doug and introduced himself.

"I bring bad tidings, princess . . . your parents . . .the King and queen . . . are dead, I'm afraid. They died when one dragon crashed into their apartments. You are now the queen, Your Majesty," he said and kneeled on his left knee.

Rebecca burst into tears, buried her face in Vinnie's chest, and held him tightly until she had the strength to stop sobbing. Captain Bedwell rose and turned to Doug.

"There are many dead and wounded in the castle. We are very grateful that Zenega and those who came with him are dead. I must return to the castle and help with the tasks ahead."

Then he looked at Audra. "My lady, I am the only senior officer left in the King's . . . ah . . . queen's guard. I assume you will become the queen's guardian until she is of legal age. Therefore, I pledge my allegiance to the queen and you and vow to protect you with my life."

"Thank you, Captain Bedwell; your words are a great comfort to Rebe . . . Her Majesty and me. We will join you shortly," Audra replied as she took Rebecca's hand.

The captain of the guard mounted his horse and headed toward the castle.

Looking at Doug, "Now, brave knight, you and your men must go quickly before the window of opportunity closes. I have kept you too long, and your future awaits you," Audra said.

"No!" Rebecca yelled. "I want Vinnie to stay." She sobbed, rushing into his arms again.

"I'm sorry, Rebecca, I can't stay. I have to return to my world with my friends. You'll be all right now. Audra will protect and guide you, and someday you will meet and marry a prince charming of your own," Vinnie said consolingly.

"I will love you forever, Vinnie," Rebecca said, tears spilling down her rosy red cheeks as she stared into his eyes.

"Audra, I don't know what to say," Doug said, taking Audra's hands in his. "I feel so strange, like I'm under a spell. But it's true; we must go . . . and quickly. How do we get back to where we came from?"

The village girls gathered around the group. They had anxiously left the shelter of the wine cellar when the last explosion occurred. They felt a need to thank the men and see them off.

"Take the road north, just past the pond, then make a left turn and follow that road. It will take you back to your world and homes,"

Audra said as she squeezed Doug's hands. Then she raised her lips to his and softly but firmly kissed him. She whispered in his ear, saying, "Farewell, my prince, till we meet again, someday in a far-off land where love is always in the air, and two hearts will beat as one." She turned and called the girls to follow her. Doug felt a strange warmth go through him. Rebecca took Vinnie's face in her hands and kissed him hard and passionately on the lips.

"Never forget me, Vinnie," she said as she followed behind Audra and the other girls. Doug, taken by surprise by Audra's words, recovered his senses.

"Okay, ladies, let's mount up and get this show on the road. As it is, we have a lot of 'splainin' to do to a less-than-receptive audience," he said apprehensively.

With great effort, the crew climbed back aboard the still-slippery tank. The men put their helmets back on and checked the intercom. Since the engine was still running, Vinnie headed toward the pond. Doug and the men filled the open hatches, and everyone waved to the women as they drove by.

Through dawn's light, Doug saw what damage the castle had sustained in the fighting as they passed. Village people and castle dwellers have gathered around, cleaning up the mess caused by the dragons and the tank. A quarter of a mile farther, Vinnie turned Vicky to the left and headed west.

The road widened and inclined steeply enough to accommodate vehicular traffic, leaving the valley behind them. Less than a mile later, the road flattened, and the terrain looked more like Colorado than where they had been. Doug spotted the old railroad station with the water tower a little further on.

"Vinnie, pull this thing under the water tower and let's get a bath. I can't stand the smell a minute longer," Doug said.

"Okay, sarge. I hope it still works," Vinnie replied.

Vinnie pulled Vicky under the water tower on the old track bed. Bailey jumped off the tank and climbed the old ladder while the rest of the crew closed the hatch covers and removed the brushes from the turret bustle. Bailey swung the water tower arm over Vicky and pulled open the stopper valve.

Water gushed over Vicky and the crew, washing the blood, guts, and body parts off the tank. While the men scrubbed the tank's surface with brushes, a group of Jeep Wranglers and pickup trucks filled with college and high school kids pulled up alongside them.

"Hey, mister," a kid yelled from the back of the first open-top jeep. "How far to the old amusement park?" He asked.

"It's less than a mile, but you will find nothing amusing if you go down there," Doug warned him.

"What's an army tank doing way out here, and what's that awful smell?" A girl with a brown ponytail asked.

"Dead dragon guts," Vinnie said. At that, the kids waved, made stupid comments, and raced off. Shortly after, Doug noticed something that caught his attention in the valley he had just left. In the distance, he heard the echoes of screams and horrified yelling.

He knew the naïve teenagers had discovered a reality they had never expected in a place that didn't exist. They had driven into the valley at the same speed; they turned around and left.

Chapter XXIII

After cleaning Vicky off, Doug ordered the crew to resume their positions. Vinnie turned over the engine and drove away from the old rail station. The air felt cool to Doug, so he allowed the hatches to remain open. He went into a mental world of his own, trying to explain the last few days' events to himself.

Vinnie turned on his cassette player. Separate Ways by Journey filled everyone's headphones and set the mood for the rest of the trip. Vinnie daydreamed about Rebecca, looking at her in his mind's eye. Doug thought about Audra and what she had said to him.

Vicky and the crew eventually made it to the south gate leading into the Fort Carson military range complex. Doug and the crew came upon another one of their company's tanks right inside the gate and over a slight rise. The crew, while getting their bedrolls secured, waved.

"What's going on?" Doug yelled to the track commander, noticing the entire company had spread out over the desert.

"Nothing, just getting ready to move out," he replied.

"No, why are we spread out over all creation?" Doug asked, clarifying his question.

"Where have you been?" The sergeant asked sarcastically.

Vinnie said over the intercom, "Hey, sarge, look. The road is muddy. It looks like they got a lot of rain."

"Where's the Third Platoon?" Doug asked the other sergeant.

"Upfront somewhere," the sergeant replied, waving his hand and arm toward the north.

"Thanks," replied Doug. "Vinnie, move us out . . . now!"

As Vinnie drove over the muddy road and across the desert, looking for the Third Platoon commander's tank, Bailey said,

"Sarge, it must still be Saturday or Sunday morning."

"My money is on Sunday morning," Boz piped in.

Doug spotted the Third Platoon leader's tank and told Vinnie to drive over to it.

"Lieutenant, we made it," Doug said, saluting Lieutenant Moore from his observation seat inside Vicky's cupola. Moore looked intently at some of his papers while he sat on the turret of his tank.

"Oh good, where did you guys end up last night?" Moore asked casually, looking up and then going back to his reading.

"Oh, we found a spot. What's on the agenda for today's activity?"

"Ah . . . I think everything's canceled for this weekend because of the weather. We will turn in the ammunition and head back after chow this morning. Did you guys eat? It's MREs today; can't set up a mess area because of the mud."

"We're fine, lieutenant. Where do you want us to park it?"

"Huh? Oh, right, there's fine," Moore said, not looking up from his sheaf of papers.

"Bingo . . . it's Sunday," chimed Vinnie over the intercom.

"Great. What will we say if someone asks us where we were?" Bailey asked over the intercom, slightly worried.

"Listen, we did what everyone else did. We bunked in the tank until the rain stopped. We were just outside the gate. That's it, got it?" Doug said with an edge in his voice.

"Hey, sarge, how are we going to account for all the spent shells, a smashed M60, and a twisted fifty cal. barrel?" Bailey asked.

"Get me an inventory of what we shot and the damage we sustained. Then we'll have to figure something out," Doug said.

"What damage, what smashed M60? Everything is in one piece! Just look for yourselves," Boz exclaimed. "The brushes we used are intact, not burned to a cinder. Even the paint job's restored!"

Bailey went to remove the first spend round, only to find it was still there. Confused, he checked the rest of them and found the same results.

"Sarge, all the rounds are here . . . intact. I don't get it," Bailey said.

"Elementary, my dear Watson. We were never there; therefore, it never happened. Ergo, no spend rounds, no damage, no explanations necessary," Boz said in an academic tone.

"Have you checked the gun tube, my dear Mr. Wakefield? I bet it's got burned residue inside the barrel," Bailey chimed.

Boz opened the breach and shined a flashlight down into the tube. "Clean as a whistle," he said smugly.

By 1500 hours, Doug watched the last tank enter through the gates of the tank park. He ordered the men to spend the rest of the afternoon cleaning up and pulling maintenance on the tank.

"All right, you men, finish cleaning up. I need to see about what, if anything, we missed," Doug said and climbed off the tank.

Doug took the weapons back to the weapon lockers and left the crew to do the chores. Vinnie, Boz, and Bailey combed the tank, looking for clues to prove that what had happened to them was real. They only found a mild odor of the dead dragon emanating from the main gun's canvas shield.

At least that's what the men thought it was . . .it was that or their imaginations. After drill, Vinnie, Boz, and Bailey went home, showered, changed clothes, and went to their favorite watering hole in Cañon City . . . Majorettes, along Freemont Avenue near Barrett Drive. It was always their tradition to go to their favorite place to hang out and have a few beers and burgers, especially after the drills.

This Sunday night brought a more somber attitude. None of the men felt like talking. The bar and grill were a combination sports bar and tavern. The back half of the place held the entire bar and three big-screen television sets mounted on the walls.

A wooden partition separated the full bar from the rest of the place.

Within wood-paneled walls and sawdust floors, the establishment arranged tables, booths, and nooks for those who merely wanted a place to meet and eat.

"She made an impression on you, didn't she, Vinnie?" Bailey said in what sounded more like a statement than a question.

Vinnie only shrugged his shoulders and took another swig from his long-necked beer bottle.

"I think Audra touched Doug, too," Boz remarked.

"We were never there; therefore, it never happened. I believe that was your quote, Mr. Wakefield," Vinnie said coolly, staring off into the distance.

"You know, Vinnie, sometimes you have no class," Boz said crossly.

"Do you mean to tell me, Vinnie, that you weren't the slightest bit captivated by Rebecca? Didn't she affect you? You don't have the slightest bit of regret that you'll never see her again?" Bailey asked.

"We were never there; therefore, it never happened," Vinnie repeated dryly.

"He's heartbroken," Boz chimed in, taking a drink of beer from his frosted mug.

Vinnie shot Boz a wild, angry look and then returned to himself. It seemed clear to Bailey and Boz that he'd struck a nerve. Something conflicting and painful continued to go on inside Vinnie. They had matured this weekend. If it hadn't happened, what had . . . and why is it affecting everybody? Vinnie understandably fought mixed emotions.

He thought he loved the girl whose only reality revolved around how to hook a husband before she was twenty-something. But Vinnie felt he was in love with the girl who never once made a demand on him and only sought his protection. This girl inherited the status of queen of her realm, but didn't exist and never existed. He was the only one to shoot a dozen people with his rifle up close and personal. That caused an onset of feelings he didn't yet understand.

The men said their goodbyes to one another and went their separate ways. Vinnie drove home in a daze, confused and unable to understand his feelings, with no one to talk to.

Monday morning brought only another ordinary day of school and work. Life as Vinnie knew it resumed again, and he lived it . . . except for the psychological changes, which caused and continued to cause unexplainable emotional turmoil within, he presumed.

The central question plaguing Vinnie was, why had he, Boz, and Bailey felt emotionally changed if it hadn't happened? They had killed countless people, destroyed a castle, used canisters on soldiers, and shot the Red Guard with machine guns.

Did this constitute a delayed stress syndrome? Or had they merely had a bad dream in their bedrolls and awakened Sunday morning as adults? But no one was talking.

Chapter XXIV

Vinnie's daydreaming halted when the professor ended the class, and the students rose to leave. The rustling of seats brought him back to reality.

He continued his mental journey through the mire he'd created, but there seemed no way out of this funk.

If he didn't pull out of it, his destiny lay in the rubble of the inevitable, sure to come crashing down. Vinnie walked out of the college building and headed toward the parking lot. He got into his car and drove to the K-Mart store in Cañon City.

He worked there every day after college classes in the Shipping and Receiving Department. Nearly two months had passed since the dynamics of his life had caused his world to change forever. When he arrived at work, he went to his station. He immediately thought about the events that had taken place since that weekend drill. Vinnie's ability to concentrate on his studies disappeared. His social skills suffered to where his parents didn't know him anymore. His only form of relief was to focus on his job. He no longer desired to have a relationship with Angela. He hadn't spoken to her since the night, a month after his last guard drill, when they'd gone out with some friends. She'd gotten on him again about getting married.

Vinnie had reached his limit. Whether his recent experience had led to this decision was hard to tell, but it was suspicious. He'd gone off on Angela like a scalded dog and told her to "Go to hell, and if I never see you again, it will be too soon. You don't have a clue what life is all about. There's more to life than fulfilling a timetable."

Naturally, she had counterattacked, screaming back, "Oh? Well, your gross immaturity causes your inability to commit yourself to anything. It shows how insecure and irresponsible you are and unfit for any woman or beast."

Vinnie had smiled broadly, his eyes agleam, and said, "Whew, I'm glad that's over. On to better things. Goodbye, Angela, and good riddance; this is it. There is no going back . . . ever." Vinnie had left Angela right where she was standing and had driven over to Majorettes.

He'd seen Bailey with friends and a girl he had recently met and was dating. Vinnie had bought a bottle of beer and joined them at their table when the girl rose to go to the ladies' room.

"Vinnie! What a surprise! We thought you were out with Angela. What's up, buddy? You look thrilled. Don't tell me . . ."

"I just broke up with Angela for good. She started on me again and just had enough," he'd said with a contorted smile.

Vinnie had shown some animation as he said this. He'd felt very excited to be free from Angela's torments. An enormous burden had flown off his shoulders; this was one less thing to contend with until he got over his funk. Bailey had been worried. He'd never seen Vinnie this way before. Maybe it was the beer. No, Vinnie said this was his first beer tonight, and he was celebrating his newfound freedom, he'd thought.

"Is that the new girl you met?" Vinnie had asked Bailey, tilting his head toward the restrooms.

"Yeah, I found her stranded on Highway 50, towed her car to my dad's shop, and fixed it for her. Naomi Crenshaw is twenty-one years old, a Chinese American, and just moved into town with her family.

"They're taking over a laundry service that her great uncle ran, who's now too old to keep it going. He wants it to stay in the family, so her father bought him out," Bailey explained.

"She's a doll, Bailey; you should hang on to this one," Vinny said.

Jonas Walker, Vinnie's boss at K-Mart, pulled him back to reality and away from his daydreaming during work.

"Vinnie, I'm short-handed on the floor. Go to the housewares department and see if you can help the customers. Explain to them that the delivery we're waiting for hasn't arrived yet. I don't need you sitting around when you can be productive elsewhere."

Vinnie went to the floor and walked through the aisles of the housewares section. As he rounded one corner, he saw the back of a tall, pony-tailed, blond-headed girl. She wore a white and blue checkered jumper over a long-sleeved, white knit sweater, opaque white tights, and black leather, calf-high boots.

She looked slim and trim. Vinnie walked up behind her, and she turned around. His eyes bulged from their sockets, and his mouth went as dry as sand. His lips hung agape, and his heart raced faster than a squirrel chasing a walnut in a cage.

He leaned forward. "Rebecca! Is it you?" He whispered, haltingly astonished.

"Yes, my name is Rebecca, but . . . do I know you?" She asked, smiling and cocking her head to one side.

Complete confusion engulfed Vinnie. He knew the Darpon thing wasn't reality or even a dream . . . or was it? His mind whirled. It didn't happen; therefore, it can't be. But her name is Rebecca, too, and she's built like her, including her excellent endowments.

"You don't look fifteen," he said rather quietly.

"I'm twenty-one . . . who are you, anyway?" She asked with a sheepish grin.

"I'm . . . my name is Vinnie . . . Vincent . . . Bolla . . . I work here. Is there something I can help you with?"

"You look like you've seen a ghost," she said, moving closer to him.

"You . . . you look like someone I met before. You could be her twin."

"Thank you; I'm flattered if that's the reaction I caused in you. Was she your girlfriend at one time?" Rebecca asked innocently.

"No, no. She was a prin . . . a friend who . . . sorta affected me, that's all. It's a long story, and . . . but you'd never believe it . . . me . . . ah . . . are you married? Have a boyfriend?" Vinnie gulped.

"No . . . and no," Rebecca said, giggling with a broader smile as she cocked her head again. "But you know, come to think of it, you look familiar. It's like we've met before. But I can't put my finger on it."

Vinnie gasped and froze for a moment after hearing that.

"Would you like to go out tonight?" He blurted, running his right hand through his black, wavy hair. He could not take his eyes off hers, those deep blue eyes she mesmerized him with.

"Sure. What time?"

Shocked by her quick response, he said, "Why don't we say about six p.m.? There are some friends I'd like you to meet."

They exchanged phone numbers. While she continued to shop, Rebecca told Vinnie she lived with her aunt and uncle. Years ago, they had retired from the Air Force and owned a home with a detached three-car garage, which had a second floor that they'd converted into a two-bedroom apartment. Until recently, they'd been renting the room to someone.

Before Thanksgiving, she had moved in from northern California. She'd worked for a software company and made good money. Unfortunately, the company closed and left her among the unemployed. She intended to pay rent when she found work locally, she said. She had come to Colorado because she preferred to live near family and liked to ski.

Vinnie called for Rebecca at 6:00 p.m. After she introduced him to her aunt and uncle, they left. Vinnie drove her to Majorettes and walked to the table where Boz and his new girlfriend sat with Bailey, his new girlfriend, and some other friends in a semicircular vinyl nook. When they stood in front of the table, the look on Boz and Bailey's faces gave away what they were thinking. They said nothing, only stared intently.

"Tell me this is not happening again," Boz whispered.

"Vinnie? Would you like to introduce your friend?" Bailey asked cautiously.

"Sure, I'd like to introduce you to Rebecca Simmons. She's living here with her aunt and uncle. Rebecca, this is Bailey Boz and Naomi. We crew and army tank together in the National Guard. I'm sorry, I don't know the name of your lady, Boz," Vinnie said.

Boz made introductions quickly and ordered more beer. Boz and Bailey exited the nook and took Vinnie to a quiet corner while the girls mingled. Vinnie explained how he'd met Rebecca that day at work. He admitted how shocked he had been.

"I brought her here because I needed to see if this girl merely amounted to a hallucination or if this was Princess Rebecca," Vinnie told them.

"She is the spitting image of the Rebecca that we remember . . . but how did she get here? Or rather, what's going on? Are there forces that we don't understand at play again?" Boz asked, and they all agreed.

Rebecca came over to the men. "From the incredulous expressions you sent in my direction, I see I garnered the same reaction from you two that I got from Vinnie this afternoon. This Rebecca you talk about must have been some babe to cause this reaction," she said, chuckling.

They both looked at Vinnie. "No, I have not told her the story yet," he assured them.

"Yes, it's quite a whopper," Boz interjected. They returned to the table.

"Speaking of whoppers, you promised me dinner, Vinnie, and I'm starving," Rebecca said with a mock pout.

Vinnie ordered food for them, along with more beer. The group partied until about 10:00 p.m. They went home because they had to get up for school and work. They agreed to meet again on Friday night.

During lunch at the college cafeteria the next day, Bailey updated Boz about the situation with his new girlfriend, having told Vinnie. Boz then told Bailey and Vinnie someone introduced him to Veronica Masters during the Thanksgiving weekend.

"I immediately became smitten with Veronica. We spent the weekend talking and getting to know each other. By Sunday, we'd become fast friends and discovered we shared a lot in common, including, but not limited to, politics and religion. Her brainpower awed me. Since then, we began dating the next weekend and have been an item."

"I'm happy for both of you. I hope it works out. At least you guys seem to have recovered better than I have. Rebecca showing up out of nowhere didn't help . . . but it didn't hurt, either," Vinnie said.

"How're things at home, Vin?" Boz asked.

"Angela keeps calling my mom and asking about me. My mom keeps beaking me about her, and I keep telling my mom it's over and to leave me alone. I told her I already had another girlfriend. That went over like a lead balloon. I'll see Rebecca as often as she'll let me," Vinnie said confidently.

"Yeah, I'm still confused about what's going on. Can we believe what this new Rebecca says?" Bailey said.

"What's the alternative?" Boz asked.

"He's right; what's the other answer? Is there one, or are we going nuts?" Vinnie asked.

"Okay, look. Darpon did not happen. We know that. Vicky returned to normal. The ammo reappeared; the damage corrected itself. The lieutenant never gave a whit where we'd been. All the evidence points to it never having happened, even though Audra said she brought us by sorcery.

"And even if that were remotely true, we're here now, and it's behind us. Rebecca is just a coincidence. It's not unrealistic to believe that a girl in this world looks exactly like her," Boz lectured.

"Yeah, all we need now is for someone who looks like Audra to show up. Then what, Einstein?" Vinnie quipped.

"Has anyone spoken to Sarge since we've been back?" Bailey asked. Vinnie and Boz shook their heads.

"We've got drill this weekend. We need to talk to him," Bailey said.

Somewhere in a far-off place, a woman looked into a pool of water. She watched her boys. She rejoiced at their newfound happiness and felt very pleased with herself. Slowly, they continued to learn the true meaning of life.

Chapter XXV

T he company commander dismissed the morning formation. The schedule for the last drill weekend before theChristmas holiday did not call to drive the tanks anywhere but for classes and medical exams at the armory. The crew walked over to Doug.

"Hey, sarge, can we talk to you?" Vinnie asked.

Doug saw a lot of torment in Vinnie's eyes, more than Boz's or Bailey's. He knew the men needed answers to many questions and feelings that had caught up to them they couldn't resolve independently. Doug knew from where they came.

He had felt the same conflicts when he returned from Vietnam. Now, he was feeling them again after the fiasco in the imaginary land of Darpon.

"Sure, c'mon. Let's go to the NCO office. I imagine you guys are dealing with a lot of confusion and emotion and want answers about what is happening inside your heads," he said.

"Mostly, that would apply to Vinnie," Bailey said. Vinnie shot Bailey a pained look.

"You're not going to believe it, sarge, but Rebecca showed up at K-Mart and messed up Vinnie's head," Boz added.

"What?" Doug asked, stopping dead in his tracks and looking at Vinnie.

As they walked across the armory floor, Vinnie filled Doug in on the details regarding Rebecca, telling him about the confusing and conflicted feelings he was experiencing and the effects they were having on him. When they got to the office, the crewmen pulled up chairs around Doug's desk.

"Did the rest of you experience issues similar to Vinnie's?" Doug asked the others.

"No, sarge, we didn't. We had questions but no answers, so we adjusted as best we could and went on," Boz replied.

"I fully understand. I had the same emotional issues and mixed feelings when I returned from the Vietnam War. I highly recommend getting some counseling. However, I will admit that the Darpon experience also affected me . . . but I have dealt with it. These things are not uncommon after experiencing battle.

"But Vinnie has an added stress. He took down a dozen men in close combat with his rifle. That can dramatically affect your psyche. Add to that stress Rebecca showing up, and you have severe internal conflicts.

"It means nothing is wrong with you, and don't start thinking there is. I believe the main conflict deals with whether it happened or not. Frankly, I admit it happened, and I believe it, but it happened in another dimension and not in our world," Doug explained.

Doug's statement put it all into perspective for Vinnie like a snap of the fingers. Now, a clear understanding electrified Vinnie's psyche for the first time. But even though Vinnie's acceptance of what happened brightened his outlook on life, it didn't account for Rebecca. Doug advised Vinnie it only amounted to a coincidence and that he should feel lucky to have met this new girl and enjoy his newfound friend.

He spoke with the crew for a while, exploring feelings and emotions and the resulting factors that had affected them. Doug played the mentor and shared his experiences dealing with post-traumatic stress disorder in more detail. He encouraged his men to call him if they had questions or problems.

The following Monday, after the weekend drill, Doug sat at his desk grading papers in his Cañon City High School office. After some time, he finally put them on his desk and stared at the wall. He needed to put things into perspective, too.

He didn't want to tell the crew of his feelings about Audra. She had made a lasting emotional impression he did not want to admit to anyone, including himself, but that he found difficult to suppress. He felt relieved that the Guard drill came and went early this December, so he didn't have to worry about it again until the middle of January.

Now, Doug could have time to concentrate on Christmas shopping and work. His parents lived in Cañon City, but his sister lived in "The Springs," as they liked to call Colorado Springs.

Over the weekend on Saturday, Doug drove to Colorado Springs. He intended to shop and visit with his sister, brother-in-law, and kids. He stopped by Citadel Mall, near his sister's home.

He parked his restored maroon 1973 Karmann Ghia in the parking lot and headed inside the mall. A few years earlier, he'd asked Bailey's father to replace the original engine with a rebuilt Porsche engine, which increased the car's performance.

He entered the mall and browsed through a department store window. He wasn't paying attention to what he was doing as Doug looked at the items. Doug accidentally bumped into a woman coming out of a candle store.

He instinctively grabbed her purchases before they slipped out of her arms and fell to the floor. In doing so, he grabbed her arm, too. He looked into her face, and just as he was about to say, "Excuse me," he went into sheer disbelief and jumped back away from her, sucking in his breath.

"I . . . I'm . . . sorry," he whispered, his eyes wild with shock.

"No, it's my fault. I wasn't watching where I was going," the woman said.

"Why are you staring at me like that?"

"You . . .you . . .look like . . .like someone I knew . . .but that's impossible," he said, trying to shake the image out of his head.

She stood there looking at him. He was still clutching her packages in both arms.

"May I have my packages back?" She asked sweetly.

"Ah . . . oh yeah . . . here." He stumbled forward and handed the packages back to her.

"Your name wouldn't be . . . be . . .Audra . . . would it?" he asked, turning his right ear toward her.

"As a matter of fact, it is. How'd you know?" She asked in a husky, friendly voice.

"Ah, it was just a chance. I knew someone who looked exactly like you," Doug explained quickly.

"There's a food court over there." She pointed. "Why don't we have some coffee? You look like you need to sit down," she said with concern.

They sat at a small table, and Doug purchased two cups of coffee. He asked, "What line of work are you in?"

"I'm a nursing supervisor at Memorial Hospital," she replied, which caused Doug to choke on a sip of coffee he'd taken. After he finished a coughing spell, he looked at her and saw, just for a split second, a pronounced twinkle in her deep brown eyes. He shook it off as an aberration.

"So, what do you do?" She asked.

"I'm a history teacher at Cañon City High School."

"What brings you to the Springs?"

"Christmas shopping and a visit with my sister. Are you married or something?" He asked, surprising even himself with his boldness.

"No, I'm not or something," she answered calmly, smiling. "You?"

"Huh . . . no . . . no, I'm not either. I almost was once, but that was a long time ago."

They sat and drank their coffee in silence, and then Doug blurted, "Would you have dinner with me tonight?"

"Well, that's fast," she said, hesitating to watch his reactions.

"Yes, I will . . . if for no other reason but to hear this wild tale."

"What wild tale?" He asked.

"The one you're dying to tell me about, this other Audra you know, met, or something."

"Yeah . . . or something," he repeated, wiping the sweat from his forehead with a napkin.

After they rose from their seats to leave, she gave Doug a broad smile, kissed him on his cheek, and squeezed his hand. He looked at her, bug-eyed and astonished, and saw another twinkle appear in her dark brown eyes for a moment and then fade away. He held her hand out to her car. His Christmas shopping was over.

EPILOGUE

On the Monday morning following the October National Guard drill weekend, a group of teenagers descended on the Colorado Springs substation of the State Patrol Office of the Department of Public Safety on Quail Lake Loop. They were there to report to a police officer an incident they had seen in a valley off Highway 115.

They told the story of coming upon an army tank at the old rail station. The tank's crew, they said, were washing dead body parts off of it with the hose of an old water tower. They related having driven into a valley where they saw a destroyed castle, devastation, damage, dead dragons, and many dead people.

They said they tried to speak with the people, but no one would talk to them. The place smelled rancid and made them all nauseated. They kept the officer's belief in what they were saying until they mentioned the dead dragons.

Now skeptical, the officer tried to appease them. Still, they were adamant it had been real, and they demanded an investigation and that something be done. The officer contacted his supervisor, who arranged for a police helicopter to fly over the area and see if there was any truth behind this story.

The teens pinpointed the old train depot's location and the valley on a state map and showed the officer where they had been. The dispatcher relayed the coordinates to the pilot. An hour later, the pilot reported that no such valley existed. He hadn't observed destroyed structures or animal remains anywhere, much less dead people. He even flew low and slow to check for unusual odors. The teens left the police building feeling confused, invalidated, and unappreciated.

They got a camera and returned to the valley to photograph what they'd seen. The teens planned to go to the nearest television station and tell their story again, but this time, they'd have pictures to prove it. They returned to the old train station later in the afternoon and noted the landmark.

They drove east along the old dirt road. The terrain remained flat and predominately hilly desert. The teens drove for an hour but never found the valley. Finally, they returned home more confused than before.

Vicky's crew remained together. They overcame the psychological issues they had experienced, helped by their girlfriends, who had met and had become close friends . . . especially Rebecca and Audra. The boys had ideas about that but didn't make it an issue. Their relationships flourished.

Doug, Vinnie, Bailey, and Boz were happily married to their respective girlfriends by the following summer. They recounted the tale of their adventure many times at their private parties. Although they told it repeatedly, no one believed them. However, Audra seemed to show a wry smile whenever she heard it. Rebecca merely giggled at Vinnie.

On Memorial Day the following year, they held a party at Doug's house. Bailey brought the bottle of Crown Royal that he'd hidden during their adventure and kept all this time for a special occasion. He decided this one was the right one. Doug applied for and got the school district administrator's job in Colorado Springs, which allowed Audra to stay at

Memorial Hospital. Vinnie moved away from his parents' house and with his wife at the apartment over his new uncle's and aunt-in-law's garage.

Boz moved to an apartment in the Springs with Veronica and got a job as an assistant professor of mathematics at the University of Colorado Extension. Bailey and Naomi lived with her parents until they found an affordable place of their own. Life was good.

Drill weekends seemed more pleasant. Everyone felt a great deal of contentment. In a faraway land, a woman looked into a pool of water and was delighted with what she saw.

About The Author

W.C. Hatounian is a twenty-four-year veteran, and a retired Army Aviator who served with the 1st Squadron, 4th United States Cavalry in Vietnam. After active duty, he joined the Arizona Army National Guard and flew with the 997th Assault Helicopter Company in Phoenix. Mr. Hatounian has always been a student of history and has read many books about military history, famous battles, and famous generals. Mr. Hatounian began his career with the Phoenix police department. After thirty-two years of service, he retired at the rank of lieutenant. He has worked in patrol during his career, flew with the department's air support unit, and headed the VICE unit and the night detective unit. Hatounian enjoys a retired life by writing books and lives in a suburb of Phoenix. He and his wife enjoy traveling and being active. He is a member of the (VHPA) Vietnam Helicopter Pilots Association. The website for his books is mynoveltales.com.

Made in United States
Orlando, FL
31 March 2025

60008931R00148